The
Rainbow
Warrior:
Genesis

C.G. Eberle

RAINBOW WARRIOR: GENESIS
Copyright © 2025 by C. G. Eberle

ISBN: 979-8-88653-305-7

Melange Books, LLC
White Bear Lake, MN 55110
www.melange-books.com

Published in the United States of America.

Cover Design by Ashley Redbird Designs

This book is dedicated to the following people:

My parents, George & Dottie Eberle, who no matter what we have been through, whether the roads have been smooth or bumpy, have shown me love and support, no matter the decisions I have made throughout my life. Thank you, Mom & Dad.

Lissa Marie Redmond who has been a friend, a colleague, and a mentor to me. I do not have the words, except thanks Lissa.

Also, I must thank my Thursday Night Writers' Group, that Lissa introduced me to, for all their support, suggestions, & critiquing. I know we do not always see eye-to-eye, but we are there to support one another, despite our differences as writers.

And most certainly my publisher Nancy Schumacher who despite the issues & difficulties I've dealt with over the past few years and am still dealing with which delayed this book. Nancy never gave up on me when she had every right to. For her support, leadership, and mentoring thank you 'Boss.'

THE ORIGIN OF THE FIVE NATIONS

Long, long ago, one of the Spirits of the Sky World came down and looked at the Earth. As he traveled over it, he found it beautiful, and so he created people to live on it. Before returning to the sky, he gave them names, called the peoples together, and spoke his parting words.

"To the Mohawk, I give corn," he said. "To the patient Oneida, I give the nuts and the fruit of many trees. To the industrious Seneca, I give beans. To the friendly Cayuga, I give the roots of plants to be eaten. To the wise and eloquent Onondaga, I give grapes and squashes to eat and tobacco to smoke at the campfires."

Many other things he told the new people. Then he wrapped himself in a bright cloud and went like a swift arrow to the Sun.

There his return caused his Brother Sky Spirits to rejoice.

PROLOGUE

F act #1: According to scientists, a seiche (/ˈseɪʃ/ SAYSH) is a standing wave in an enclosed body of water. The most vital necessity for a seiche, is the body of water needs to be at least partially enclosed, allowing the formation of the standing wave, and they are customarily born when strong winds and rapid changes in atmospheric pressure push water from one end of a body of water to the other. When the wind stops, the water ricochets to the other side of the enclosed area. The water then continues to swing back and forth for hours or even days. On a small scale this can be seen in teacups, bathtubs, and swimming pools. On much larger scales this happens in lakes, as in the Great Lakes.

Lake Erie is known for seiches, especially when strong winds begin to blow southwest to northeast, which is what happened on October 18th, 1844. According to reports and the local media, a twenty-two-foot wall of water overflowed the lower districts of Buffalo, NY destroying many buildings, devastating a large area of the harbor front, and creating mayhem for the shipping industry. The Black Rock neighborhood was flooded with anywhere from two to eight feet of water. On the city's east side, the water came as high as Seneca Street just below Michigan Avenue and completely covered the area. An accurate count of the dead was impossible to attain, due to a large number of homeless and destitute who were on the streets, and in the waterfront, who were swept back into Lake Erie, but at least seventy-five people were believed killed.

Fact #2: Calcite's a crystalline mineral, and it's been used in Ancient Egypt in carvings related to some of their goddesses. Nowadays it's used in soil remediation and stabilization, and in concrete repair. During the Second World War, the United States Government took a great interest in the element for research and weapons' development. Recently it was discovered a massive vein of calcite is under the Cattaraugus Indian Reservation in Western New York, unknown to the residents living there.

Separately, these details were minor bits of trivia for most, but eventually outside forces would forge a new path for a young man seeking his past, all leading to his destiny.

ONE

Alex Harlow was staggered, and words escaped him. The man didn't know how to respond or what to think, to the news he'd been waiting to hear. Finally, after a moment or two of stunned silence Alex was able to squeak out, "Miss Guthrie, could you say that again?" as he clutched his cordless phone, in a choking grip.

"Certainly Mr. Harlow," a pleasant, almost sympathetic voice replied. "The state will be releasing copies of your files to my office, and we should be receiving your adoption records sometime next week. This means we will be one step closer to reuniting you with your family."

Alex didn't know that his caseworker, Marie Guthrie, was forced to pull the handset away from her left ear due to his overzealous "ALL RIGHT!"

"Oh my God! That's the best news I've gotten since...I

don't know," he told her with eyes wide open and his heart pounding. Alex began pacing around his living room, practically jumping. "You've no idea what this means," he added, then nervously asked, "So, any idea when I'll actually see the records?"

At first, he heard papers being shuffling around, then his caseworker said, "Let me check here." Alex presumed Marie was checking her hanging Lil' Woofers Puppy calendar, he'd seen when he came into the Homeward Angels office for his in-person meetings. She drummed her knuckles on her desk loud enough for Alex to hear. "Barring a clerical glitch, I'd say within a week, give or take, knock on wood. Once I receive a confirmed date, I'll call you so we can set aside some time."

His stomach felt like it was corkscrewing around like a roller coaster. "You don't understand what this means to me," he said, then he clenched up his right fist hard enough that all his knuckles crack on their own and sounded like shelled nuts being split open. It was a habit Alex acquired to fight off nervousness or to keep anger under control when needed.

"I wanna thank you for all the help you gave me this past year." He stopped to let out a soft brief laugh. "Hell, I'd still be trying to figure out the paperwork for the appeals process with the state." Then, uncharacteristically, Alex leapt without looking. "I'd like to find a way to thank you."

"That isn't necessary Mr. Harlow, I've only been doing my job."

Alex imagined Marie had similar discussions from past clients who wanted to show their appreciation, but claim it was against Homeward Angels policy to accept gratuities, as a way to defuse uncomfortable situations, especially if it was more of a case of male hormones overriding common sense. Being fifty years old, Alex had dealt with similar situations, but now he knew how to handle moments like these. Yes, his caseworker was attractive, and he wanted to show her his gratitude, but that's where it ended. By this point in his life, Alex didn't cross certain lines.

"I get it," he quickly chimed in. "But I don't think you realize what this means, let me try to explain." Alex needed a moment to arrange his thoughts and once he knew what he wanted to say, he continued. "Maybe someone else could say it more articulately, but when you're adopted, you're on one side of the fence or the other; either you don't care about your biological family or have a need to know. For me I've always been the latter. I've felt this need since I was a kid and thanks to you, I'm a step closer to finding out the truth."

Alex realized Marie had become silent and wasn't sure what it meant. It didn't feel 'uncomfortable' to him, but he didn't know what she was thinking. Marie then asked, "What do you mean?"

"I'll try to clarify it for you. I always felt incomplete, like a jigsaw puzzle with the outer edges and most of the inside finished, but several vital central pieces missing. Without them you'll never get the whole picture. Because of your help, my picture's gonna be a little more filled in. Whether good or bad, I'll know more than I do now, and trust me even if my biological family doesn't want me around, knowing's better than not knowing."

After a moment of silence, Alex heard the understanding in Marie's voice, and more empathy than she'd ever shown before. He could tell by the warmth in her tone. "Mr. Harlow I understand," she said softly. "Across the street from my office is the West Seneca library building, inside's a Spot Coffee, I admit I'm very fond of Chai tea."

"I know it—been there several times since my mom's a

librarian there. Name the time and the tea and brownies are on me. And it's Alex."

"All right, Alex, I'll let you know but only if you call me Marie, agreed?"

"Sound doable, Marie."

———

After hanging up, Alex sat down on the beige love seat in his living room, nearly collapsing since he was still in shock, and he wasn't sure what surprised him more; the news or reaching out to Marie the way he did.

Beyond grateful, Alex's luck seemed to finally be changing for the better. Over the past few years, he faced several setbacks and regrets that still plagued him, and Alex frequently wondered when he became a punching bag for the universe.

To the world at large he seemed fine, truth was he kept things hidden and wore a mask. His anger and depression he hid from almost everyone, because there were days when he was overwhelmed by the emotions. They towered above him, making some days unbearable emotionally speaking. But somewhere deep inside there was a trace of hope, telling him to keep fighting to the last round, to keep swinging, even when the final bell is rung. For whatever reason Alex kept listening and didn't submit when the abyss he stared into stared back at him. Somehow, he defiantly stood his ground and spit in its eye.

Alex tried to process everything, from the very beginning. When Alex was less than a year old, he had been adopted by Reggie and Celeste Harlow, and when old enough to understand what that meant, they explained everything to him. From an early age Alex knew his biological mother couldn't raise him but loved him enough to make certain he'd go to a good family. That also meant Alex had unanswered questions, the key one being why? Like he told Marie he was an incomplete jigsaw puzzle.

Alex's thoughts switched from a mishmash of eagerness & expectations to concern, when he realized he'd no idea how to break the news to his parents. They always supported his natural curiosity regarding his biological family, when he reached out to the state, and finally going to Homeward Angels, whose mission was to reunite families that were separated for various reasons. No matter what he said, or how Alex told them, he knew the Harlows would be shaken up, particularly Celeste. He just had to figure out a way to tell them, without it being a verbal slap to the face.

While he sat there, in a perplexed state for a few minutes, Alex finally realized his stomach had been snarling like a wild animal, sounding like a growling wolverine or badger, which wasn't surprising since he hadn't eaten since breakfast, and knew he'd better figure out what to make for dinner. With his parents out at their monthly cousins' luncheon, the man knew he'd be cooking for one.

Alex stood up, rubbed the back of his neck, attempting to massage out the tension he felt, which is when his peripheral vision caught sight of something he'd recently seen several times, and he momentarily forgot about everything else. Through the sheer, semitransparent curtains hanging in front of his living room window, Alex saw a dark blue SUV, the same one he'd sporadically seen for the past two weeks.

Alex first noticed the SUV about two and a half weeks ago, parked at various points on his block. At first, he didn't think anything about it, figuring one of the neighbors got a new truck, or someone had company, but things didn't add up; the frequency of days, with some weekdays, some weekends, and the SUV was never in any of the driveways, always parked on the winding block, within proximity to the Harlow home.

Alex's instincts kicked in. His mother always said Alex had a sixth sense stronger than anyone she knew, let alone heard of, and this was one of those times the man listened to his instincts more than his common sense. Something about the SUV bothered Alex and he followed his gut.

In a previous life the one-level, ranch style house, had been a local doctor's office, while she lived in the original half of the house, the nine-room wing add on, became her office/exam rooms. When his parents bought the property, it was being sold as a three-bedroom, with an in-law suite. After Alex moved back in to help them with the property and chores, he had the doctor's offices as his own half of the house.

Alex exited from his own private entrance, alongside the Harlow's two-car garage, that was attached to his wing of the house. He walked down the four-car driveway, past his, steel-blue, gun metal, Charger right towards the sidewalk at a casual pace. As he headed through the glaring, white sunlight, into the cool, darkening shadow from his neighbors' towering pine tree, that cut across the street, Alex's glare tightened up, and became laser focused.

Once he stepped onto the blacktop, the SUV's engine roared to life without warning, then pulled away from the curb at what seemed a dangerous rate of speed for the quiet neighborhood.

As a cool, fall breeze began gusting, Alex watched the truck head towards Lackawanna, right on the border of Alex's neighborhood, and thought *Glad no kids playing out here*, because there'd be no way the driver could have stopped if anyone was in the street.

His mind went somewhere between curiosity and concern. Nothing screamed "DANGER" to him, but no one entered the SUV, which suggests the driver had been sitting there for some time, and Alex's mind started to come up with possibilities. *Could've been on their cell or checking their email. Maybe they were trying to decide what radio station to pick. There could have been a fussy kid in the backseat a parent had to deal with, or just be a coincidence, yeah, a coincidence.* As Alex ran down the options, and knew it was all bunk: everyone who knew him knew how he felt about coincidences.

———

Back inside Alex did the only thing he could think of, start dinner. Cooking would help him calm down. For Alex, cooking was a form of therapy, because no matter what else was going on, when he baked, roasted, or broiled something, everything changed for him, he slowed down his thinking, his breathing, the way he did almost everything, bordering on a meditative state.

Alex decided on Asian chicken with Chinese veggies for dinner and soon had some sesame oil heating up in his copper skillet. As the aroma of chicken, seasonings, soy sauce, and veggies filled the kitchen, the clock radio, which sat on the top of the stainless-steel refrigerator, played the classic hit, *You're the Inspiration* by Chicago, when Alex heard the familiar, earsplitting alert, usually reserved for Emergency Broadcast Tests. He stopped, cold, at the announcement.

"We interrupt this program; this is an emergency alert for Erie, Pennsylvania to the Downtown Buffalo, New York region. A massive wave of water coming from Lake Erie is expected to reach downtown Buffalo, New York between 5:10 and 5:13 p.m. eastern standard time. Authorities advise anyone along the Lake Erie shoreline to stay away from the lakefront due to massive cresting waves. Authorities are advising those downtown to vacate Canalside, the Harbor Center, Buffalo Riverworks, the Time Beach Nature Preserve, the Buffalo Naval & Military Park, and the Cobblestreet District. The skyway and Route 190 to and out of downtown are being closed off. Route Five leading downtown is being closed off at Tift Street."

Alex didn't realize his grip slipped and dropped his large, black spatula. His jaw went slack as the message repeated itself, and finally he snapped out of his stunned state, ran through the dining room, and into the living room to turn on his flat screen. Standing in front of the T.V., in stunned silence, Alex just watched the scene play out, as the news anchors tried to explain everything as it happened.

Live shots showed police cars blocking off the Skyway at the foot of Church Street, then the image switched to the cameras mounted on top of the Seneca One Tower, looming over Main Street. The new shot showed cresting white caps, rolling all over Lake Erie and the Buffalo River, coming into the shoreline, near the General Mills plant, Canalside, and the Buffalo Naval Park, where the USS Sullivans, USS Little Rock, and the USS Croaker all sat defenseless in port.

"As you can see from our Channel Two cameras mounted on the Seneca One Tower," the female anchor said, "White caps are already forming, and the water is choppy down by the boat harbor and the waterfront. The National Weather Service has issued a small craft advisory and although it's late in the season, the advisory is normally used for wind gusts, but there still boat owners with craft on the water, at the Erie Basin Marina, as well as at the Buffalo Small Boat Harbor, near Gallagher Beach, but the authorities are ordering no one to be on the water until after this event passes and they declare the area safe. The Coast Guard and the Erie County Sheriffs are monitoring for anyone attempting to violate the order by helicopter and have informed Channel Two anyone caught violating the order will be detained and arrested."

Alex finally sat down, almost crumpling into his leather recliner without taking his eyes off the screen. He watched as the camera panned and the image focused on the lighthouse on Fuhrmann Boulevard, near the Coast Guard Station.

A male co-anchor then said, "We already know this is a severe situation, but it may be more serious than anyone believed at first. Right now, we're looking at a live shot of the historical Buffalo Main Lighthouse on Fuhrman Boulevard, which is emitting a pulsating light in all directions. These lights act as a beacon to alert the region's superhero community, to where they are needed. At present none of the local heroes have been seen on site, but with the beacon sending out a summoning signal, it's almost guaranteed heroes such as Republic Steele the hero from World War Two, and local teams like the South Buffalo based Garda will be on site as soon as possible."

The site of the lighthouse gave Alex a chill that ran from the core of his stomach and he had a good reason to feel this way. In a flash remembering when he was six or seven years old, Alex's family was near the historical landmark, when the beacon lights sent out the signal, but this time the entity linked to the phenomenon materialized, and Alex saw him. An apparition, who appears as a spectral lighthouse keeper, that's been an urban legend since the 17th century, named Ghostlight, materialized in front of Alex during some superhuman battle that was taking place near the lighthouse. Alex could only remember bits and pieces, and the details were scattered, but when Ghostlight appeared to Alex and his parents, he stared at the boy. At first Alex was terrified, but soon felt safe, when in a moment the phantom somehow shielded the family from the conflict. Every time he saw the beacon light or the lighthouse, Alex relived those moments in his mind.

As the camera panned, then focused on the eight-sided tower of stone blocks, topped with the gallery deck on the outside and the lantern room inside, Alex just watched the pulsating light wondering who was being summoned and how bad things were about to get.

TWO

After hanging up Marie sat in her tan and gray cubical smiling, then let out a small laugh at how Alex took the news. She playfully twirled a length of her long brown hair, with her left index finger, an unconscious habit she'd had since the age of ten or eleven years old, but rarely thought about, unless she caught herself doing it.

A warm, pleasant feeling rose from within her, and Marie knew it came from Alex's reaction, then she thought *Definitely unexpected, but it's nothing I can't handle. Not like this is the first time, but agreeing is.* It'd come up before; clients, co-workers, even her mailman once, and Marie always handled these moments with tact and grace, but this time the native Californian was curious to see where the winds would take her. Even though Alex was about fifteen years her senior, her intuition told her Alex wasn't like the others, with one thing on their minds. Besides Marie admitted to herself there was something intriguing about the man, her curiosity was peaked.

Without thinking Marie began drumming her rose colored fingertips on her desk, staring at her phone, without really looking at it. She understood the desperation people felt when searching for lost family members, there were numerous reasons. The reasons were almost as infinite as the stars, but when it came to Alex, Marie somehow knew it was more. All her life Marie listened to her instincts, some call it a sixth sense or women's intuition, it didn't really matter, she learned a long time ago to trust it.

Marie came back to reality when she heard a teasing voice say, "So, you're looking pleased with yourself."

She looked over the top of her cubicle and saw her co-worker and best friend Midge smiling down at her. "Have a nice conversation," she asked. "Finally get a date?"

Marie blew her a raspberry loud enough to echo throughout the building. "As a matter of fact, yes I had a pleasant phone call, thank you for asking," then the native Californian slipped her dark gray loafers back on.

"Ooh," Midge said leaning up against the cubical side, teasing some more. "Okay give, who you are going out with? I need details girl."

"Well, nosey, I just informed one of my clients we're getting his files next week, as if that's any of your business," she mocked.

It was Midge's turn to blow a raspberry. "Just curious. I saw you smiling, it got me wondering," the twenty-some-thing coyly said as she selected a couple of chocolate candies from Marie's blue & white porcelain candy dish.

Being early fall with late summer weather and a chance of rain, Marie had opted to bring a light sweater to fight any potential chill that was possible, which she tied around her neck, over her light blue blouse. She rose from her office chair, and when Marie stood it was clear she was at least a head and a half taller than Midge. "So who's the client?" Midge asked as she unwrapped a chocolate.

Marie secured her computer, then packed up her work

bag with her work laptop, active files, and a few other items. "Alexander Harlow, we're a step closer to finding his family."

"Oh yeah, I remember him," Midge said, "Very not bad," she added, sounding like she was reviewing a male stripper show. "A few years older than you, but I'll be he can show a woman a good time."

Marie just shook her head, knowing Midge's style. "It's not like that."

"Really," Midge taunted, "good to know since I've been in a bit of drought myself lately. So, you don't have a problem next time he comes in, if I see if he'd like to go out for drinks and finger foods at The Border," Midge light-heartedly asked referring to a nearby tavern. Marie just gave Midge her best scornful, motherly look, then finished locking up her desk. "So, where you off to?" Midge asked as she unwrapped her second piece of candy.

"Downtown, I have to attend the monthly meeting," Marie said.

"Right," Midge said. "Now getting back to that smile girlfriend, you haven't smiled like that since I've known you. So come on, give." She popped another chocolate in her mouth.

Marie slightly blushed. "There's nothing to give," she said as she picked up her work bag and threw it over her shoulder, then moved towards the vestibule, saying goodbye to some of her coworkers, with Midge following like an overexcited puppy.

As Marie reached the inner glass doors, she heard Midge say, "Come on, ever since you moved here, it's always home and work for you. You rarely come out with us to The Border after work or have any kind of social like. It's good to see you happy."

Marie stopped at the outside glass and metal door,

turned to her younger colleague. "When did you take an interest in my dating life, Mother?"

As she was about to head out the door, Marie felt Midge grab her wrist, looked back and saw Midge's manner change. She wasn't kidding around, the five foot, even brunette with warm tone ribbons in her hair said, "It's just cause I care, you're almost like family. And you don't have anyone here, actual family, I mean."

Knowing where Midge was coming from, Marie appreciated her friend's concern, and she hugged her. "I understand what you're saying about socializing and 'getting a life'. It's just that I'm busy here helping the clients or something always comes up. There never seems to be enough time, but I promise next time the crew heads out I'll be there."

"All right," Midge responded pointing her index finger at Marie. "But I'm holding you to that." With that Marie waved goodbye and headed to her blue mini-Cooper.

On the outside she was fine, but inside Marie felt cold since she knew Midge's words rang true. Except for her work 'family' and a few connections, she didn't have anyone close to her. As she thought about what Midge said, the memories flashed back.

Three years ago, Marie had been living just outside of San Diego, with her parents Devon and Amber Guthrie, planning her future, when a car crash killed her parents, and everyone said it was a miracle Marie survived, but obviously her life changed forever. After some time passed, she'd been able to finally put things in order and felt she needed a fresh start, in a new city. Not only was Marie looking to turn the page, but she knew she needed to close the book and begin a new one.

Marie had been working at Homeward Angels back in San Diego, when she heard of an opening in the Buffalo,

New York area, applied for the position, and in less than two months she was on her way to Western New York and her new life.

Marie was happy with her work at Homeward Angels, with their mission being to aid people who were searching for family members who'd run away, walked away, seemingly vanished, or were given away, like Alex was or those who wanted to come home. Helping those in need is what gave Marie her true pleasure, her purpose in life, it was her passion. In her five and a half years with the agency Marie had been able to help reunite thirty families, now hopefully it'd soon be thirty-one.

———

Marie took the fastest route to downtown Buffalo, from the suburbs right into the heart of the city. Except for an occasional eighteen-wheeler, delivery truck, or senior driver that drove too slow for the 190, the drive was uneventful, and she had time to clear her head. Marie knew Midge meant well, but there were times she could be as blunt as a sledgehammer to the skull. Finally, Marie's thoughts shifted from what she'd lost three years ago to what she might be gaining.

Somehow Marie knew there was more to Alex than she realized when they first met. In time she saw what kind of man Alex was when he came to the office and her instincts said she could trust him. Finally, Marie realized she wanted to see Alex away from the office and Midge had been right all this time. Reaching out might be worth the risk.

———

It took Marie over twenty minutes and traffic got heavier the closer she got to the historic Cobblestone District, and she had to begin tapping her brakes more and more. *Maybe I'd should have taken Seneca,* Marie thought as she exited the 190 and cruised past the Pierce Arrow Museum. In less than five minutes Marie pulled into the parking lot for Homeward Angels downtown location, almost directly under the skyway and near the fully restored Buffalo Heritage Carousel from 1924. As Marie headed inside the one story, brick building, nearly a century old, she braced herself, mentally. Marie didn't hate the monthly meetings, but she tolerated them because they weren't the most engaging part of her job, being an assistant manager. Reviewing quarterly reports, HR issues, companywide updates, policy changes, and various future projects or plans, including an upcoming holiday party. Not the most exciting way to spend an afternoon, but she'd come to accept it was part of the job.

Marie was getting bored because the agenda included changes in the hiring policies and planning for the upcoming company Christmas party, which everyone was looking forward to, but she'd heard it all before. Marie listened carefully, occasionally asking questions or taking notes, but she was already looking forward to taking a long, hot soak in her tub once she got home.

District manager, Jeremy Nicholas, tried to wind things up. "Okay folks, I know it's getting late, and we've one more thing to go over. It's nothing major, but it has to do with the annual holiday charity we'll be donating to this year," he began saying, when a female associate broke protocol and sprinted into the meeting room, without knocking.

The young, dark skinned woman from India, with a British accent apologized, then quickly explained. "There is an emergency alert coming over the telly in the break room. The authorities have ordered everyone to evacuate this area immediately! A massive wave is coming off Lake Erie and headed this way!"

One of the women who sat opposite Marie, facing the floor-to-ceiling windows, bolted up pointing at the windows towards the lake and the waterways. Everyone instinctively turned and stared at the spectacle, stampeding towards them.

Everyone watched, horror on their faces as a rolling wave stormed in past Wilkeson Point, past the Outer Harbor channel, aiming right for the Skyway. The rolling waters, white capped at the top, seemed to be gathering speed with each passing second, and gathered mass and power, with a height rarely seen. The seiche towered over the office and the surrounding area, swallowing up everything in its path, being a force of nature that was devouring more, looking like it'd never end.

For Marie and her colleagues there wasn't time to move, or react, or even think. The people inside the office did one of two things; freeze in place with fear or run out of pure panic. Marie fell into the category of the former as the seiche rolled into downtown Buffalo like the Wrath of God was unleashed.

THREE

C harlie Beck wasn't far from Marie and her colleagues when they started their meeting. The bookish, studious man was anxiously waiting at the corner of Seneca Street and Michigan Avenue, although he looked as calm as a stone Buddha on the outside, internally the man's stomach was churning up enough stomach acid to melt a concrete rebar.

Beck stood outside of the Department of Environmental Conservation office, across the street from the Pierce-Arrow Museum, then suddenly felt a spritzing of small raindrops on his head and at the back of his neck. Beck hoped his ride would arrive before any real downpour would happen. As he looked up at the gray skies, with darker clouds, moving in from the north he thought *Just my luck to get soaked my last day here.*

Life had never unfolded as Beck had hoped or planned. The diminutive man, with his white-gray hair and Buddy Holly style glasses, found that life's opportunities were either snatched away or simply bypassed him too often. Sometimes, they didn't materialize as they did for others.

But finally, at last the brass ring was within his grasp, and Beck was resolute in seizing it.

For the past twenty-three years Beck worked as an environmental analyst for the D.E.C. He took water and earth samples, explored, examined, and evaluated meteorological data. His supervisors told him he was essential to their work, but finally, after two decades of this work, Beck felt it was a meaningless, pointless job, which capped off his meaningless, pointless life, and he was looking to get out by any means.

He stood on the corner staring at the car museum, that opened in 2001 and showcased Buffalo's transportation history featuring the Pierce Arrow, the Thomas Flyer, vintage electric vehicles and bicycles, with motorcycles, muscle cars and trucks, the majority manufactured in the Buffalo region. The museum of luxury cars was one of the only things Beck liked about his job at the D.E.C. He'd regularly tour the museum of classic cars on his lunch breaks or after work. When he visited, Beck obsessively stared at the collection with envious eyes. It wasn't that Beck desired to possess the collection itself or harbor a passion for classic cars, it's what they represented; money which equaled freedom, freedom Beck never had.

Fresh out of college, he found himself bound to his ailing parents, then to a woman who assumed he'd marry her, just because they'd dated in college a few times. Eventually, he reached his limit and harshly severed ties with her, declaring he couldn't bear her presence any longer. Finally, he'd been chained to a job he'd grown to hate, but that was all about to change. Goodbye to the D.E.C., co-workers he hated, bad coffee, reports, collecting samples, and most of all goodbye to Western New York, forever. Now that Beck was finally an orphan there were no obstacles left to prevent him from making a fresh start.

Beck wasn't just killing time after another lousy work-day; he'd been instructed to wait outside his office to complete a delivery and he intended to follow those orders, get his pay off, and finally start a new life.

The afternoon was cloudy and grey, with storms approaching from Canada as forecasted, prompting Beck to wear his raincoat over his best grey suit. A sudden, powerful gust off the lake caught Beck's open raincoat, giving the illusion that he was exposing himself to the passing cars. Beck's focus quickly moved from merely clutching his worn mahogany brown attaché case and contemplating his future, to closing his raincoat while keeping a death grip on his briefcase.

Rush-hour traffic began flowing, taking workers home, while Beck scanned along Michigan Avenue desperately looking for his ride. After numerous cars passed by for what seemed a remarkably lengthy time, a two-tone black and pearlized gray luxury car finally pulled up to the corner on Seneca, screeching to a dead stop startling Beck.

The tinted, passenger's side window rolled down with a whisper of a hum, the female driver leaned over and said, "Mr. Beck, get in."

Beck was astonished to see an attractive, young female chauffeur beckoning to him. He approached the front passenger door, only to find it locked. "Please, take the back seat," the driver instructed, before the window swiftly closed.

Beck reached for the rear passenger door, climbed inside, and sat down. The inside of the car reminded Beck of a mausoleum, it felt cold, dark, and quiet. After Beck's vision adjusted to the car's interior lighting, he knew something was off, and asked "Where's Mr. Rollins, he told me he'd be takin' care of the exchange.".

The young female driver said in an almost harmonious

voice, "Mr. Rollins is unavailable. I am taking you to meet with Mr. Segel."

Ohmigod! Beck was suddenly gripped by alarm due to the unexpected change in plans. For Beck, a lack of control was intolerable; he firmly believed that once plans were made, they should be set in cement. But experience taught him the necessity of flexibility, especially when dealing with those paying the freight. When they said jump, they expected to see air under one's feet. Beck's anxiety turned to pure fear because he'd been expecting to hand off all the records and files of an inquiry regarding a mineral report done at the Cattaraugus Reservation near Irving, New York.

Once Beck closed the door, the BMW made a hairpin turn onto Michigan Avenue, merging with the rushing flow of traffic, accelerating and overtaking several vehicles by skillfully weaving in and out of lanes. leaving them all look like they were stuck in quicksand. From the passenger seat, Beck saw streets fly by, then at the foot of Michigan the BMW banked a hard left onto Ohio Street, which bounced Beck around like a pinball for a moment.

"Where we headed?" Beck asked apprehensively.

The driver said, "To a private meeting site, nearby, Mr. Beck. It's not far."

Especially with the way you're driving, he thought.

As the car sped down Ohio Street, Beck struggled to recognize his surroundings due to the high speed, reckless driving, and dark window tint. Eventually, he recognized the General Mills plant on his right, and shortly after, they crossed the Ohio Street bridge. Beck wondered how the driver had managed to avoid any red lights but suspected she must've run several.

Crossing the Buffalo River, the BMW proceeded along Ohio Street, running parallel to the Skyway. Weaving through the thickening traffic, the driver's audacity made Beck question her sanity, particularly when she pulled into the oncoming lane, narrowly avoiding a head-on collision by swerving sharply to the right, forcing a panel van to blast its horn in angry protest.

"How much longer?" Beck asked, sounding queasy.

"We're just about there," was her only response.

Finally, the luxury car slowed down, cut to a side road, then it made a left after passing the water treatment plant. Beck recognized the area; they were next door to the Tift Nature Preserve, an urban nature reserve with over two hundred and sixty acres of trails, antiquated boardwalks, and seventy-five-acres of marsh, home to scores of wildlife, and a visitors' site that was popular year-round, all right between downtown and South Buffalo.

The car came to a near crawl and Beck knew they were close. "We're here, Mr. Beck," the driver announced, as if she were headed up a sightseeing tram ride, but he didn't need to be told.

Beck looked out the windshield and felt himself stop breathing because standing before him was Regino Segel, the fifty-five-year-old magnate, and the Chief Operating Officer of his family's conglomeration, Segel International, and the man was rumored to be worth three quarters of a billion dollars.

The BMW halted abruptly four hundred yards beyond a road fork, and as the driver turned to face Beck, he noticed she was an attractive, early thirty-something, with a variation of a pixie hairstyle, dyed cobalt blue complemented by matching lipstick. "Mr. Segel is waiting for you," then the doors unlocked with a noticeable click.

Beck stepped out tentatively, his briefcase at his side, still in his death grip. He walked around the front of the BMW, trying to avoid a few muddy puddles between the cars, as the wind began kicking up and the sprinkles now felt like a misty rain coming down lightly.

It was then Beck saw a towering figure: a bald African American man with very dark skin, who Beck estimated weighed at least three hundred and seventy pounds and stood about six feet ten inches tall was standing off to the side, next to another BMW, that was a twin of the one he arrived in.

Beck walked over the dirt road, feeling heavier and more nervous with each step as he approached Segel, a man younger than him, only in his mid-fifties. Beck realized Segel was giving him a piercing stare and an expectant smile. The tall, well-built man, with salt-and-pepper, spiked hair and a matching Van Dyke beard, was impeccably groomed, wearing a stylish charcoal gray suit, which was typical for him. Segel exuded confidence. His attitude was self-assured, bordering on arrogant, with a touch of charisma that drew people in. Beck thought that could be one of the reasons he agreed to sell out, that and the money.

Finally, on the grassy part of the road, face to face, Beck said, "Mr. Segel, I uh thought... I thought I would be meeting with Mr. Rollins again."

Segel, responded as he extended his gloved right hand. "Indeed, Mr. Rollins is engaged in a special project for me, so I thought it prudent to oversee this matter personally." Segel, with a fleeting smirk, glanced at the worn briefcase and gave a slight nod before inquiring, "Are those the reports you were asked to bring?"

"Ah, yeah...yes sir," Beck answered while weakly shaking hands and instinctively he clutched the briefcase closer to his side. "It's everything Mr. Rollins asked for; the D.E.C.'s reports and the computer records, both hard copies and the downloads on the flash drive he gave me. Everything." Beck then took a hard swallow, as his mouth began to dry itself out. "Now, when my superiors discover that the records have been copied and my reports are missing, they will start searching for me, so I have to leave tonight."

"No need to worry about that; the thumb drive you used has a special program embedded on it. Once you copied the information, the program launched a virus that destroyed all traces of the files I needed."

"You mean…" Beck began to speak as he comprehended what Segel was saying.

"Of course, your former employers will know something is missing, but there won't be any evidence of anything nefarious. Naturally, they will want to speak with you, so I understand you're anxious to get on with your plans. I won't keep you." Segel spoke as he began to walk back into an area with denser coverage. "Walk with me," he instructed.

Being early October, several trees in the region already shifted colors from various shades of greens to red, oranges, and gold, but the fall foliage hadn't reached peak coverage, yet. "Being you are leaving, you should get a final look around, while you can. This is a beautiful area this time of year, I can see why people love it so much."

Nervously Beck said, "Ah, I gotta be honest, Mr. Segel I don't really care about that. I just want my money, then to get to the airport."

As they approached Beth Pond, which was on the far side of Tift Farms, Segel turned and continued. "That's a mistake Mr. Beck." Then he paused looking over the nature preserve in front of them. "My father taught me a lot; one lesson was one should take time to appreciate the simple pleasures in life. He told me that, just before he died."

Beck's stomach plummeted and suddenly he wanted out of this deal but knew there was no way out. "Here you go, now about my money," Beck asked handing over the briefcase.

Examining it with a fresh look of eagerness and expectation, Segel took it in both hands, then asked, "So everything is here?"

Beck shook his head in disbelief at what he was doing, the doubts rose up on him, like a sudden wave of nausea. "Yeah," he said as he looked around at the grounds and the huge pond, where a pair of mallards were swimming. "Everything, all materials related to the mineral rights tests done at the Cattaraugus Reservation, as asked for."

"Excellent," Segel said, still staring at the briefcase.

"So, Mr. Segel, if that's all?" Beck asked.

"Of course, Mr. Beck, you have places to go." Behind Segel, Macaria, the female driver, came up behind him, like a stalking panther. "If you would," Segel said, and handed the briefcase to her.

"Yes sir," was all she said, then backed away to the BMW she and Beck arrived in.

Confused, Beck was tempted to demand his money but thought better of it.

"I've your payoff right here Mr. Beck," Segel said, nodding towards his huge driver. Without a word the male chauffeur walked over to them, as he reached into his dark gray sportscoat, and pulled out an envelope.

Beck watched in a silent panic, because he thought for a moment the assistant was going to pull out a gun and shoot him. Relief washed over Beck when Segel said "Jacob has your new identity documents; birth certificate, social-security card, credit cards, driver's license, everything you'll need, and a one-way ticket to Vancouver. Rollins mentioned you were planning to leave the country, first to Canada then parts unknown, but you hadn't made your flight arrangements, so I took the liberty. I think you will find the payment adequate. You will also find the new account information set up in your new identity at the CIM Banque of Switzerland. Once established, I'd contact their representatives as soon as possible."

Taken aback Beck wasn't sure what to say as he took the envelope from Jacob except "Thank you, Mr. Segel."

Beck felt Segel place his free hand on his back, persuasively, then he guided him back towards the BMW Jacob was standing by. "My pleasure Mr. Beck, Jacob will first take you to your residence to get your things, then drive you to the airport. You have a nine forty-five Air Canada flight first to Toronto, then straight on to Vancouver. You, or I should say Mr. Jerry Peters is booked into an exclusive cabin, I hope that is acceptable." Segel smiled artfully and even though Beck's anxiety level dropped, the look on Segel's face reminded Beck of a predator eyeing prey on Animal Planet.

Beck said "Thank you very much Mr. Segel. I don't know what to say," then Segel took his glove off and extended his right hand again, barring an onyx & gold ring.

As they shook hands, Segel said, "There's nothing left to say, except have a good journey."

———

After Segel instructed Jacob to drive Beck home, he watched the luxury car pull away at a more leisurely pace than when Beck arrived. As the vehicle quickly vanished from sight, Regino sensed Macaria approaching from behind with her cat-like grace. She queried, "You didn't really mean that, did you? About wishing him a good trip, I mean."

Without taking his eyes off the car as it disappeared out of sight Regino said, "Of course I did, I meant every word." He briefly paused, turned to face his personal chauffeur /bodyguard, and looked into her in her catlike violet eyes, then continued. "I know Beck will have a fine trip. Jacob will take care of things and by the time Beck is found, he will have been in the Niagara River for some time, up near Lake Ontario, perhaps in the gorge or the lake itself, depending on the flow currents." As Regino headed towards the BMW he directed Macaria, "If you'd drive us home now, I've a transfer of funds to reverse and some serious reading to do."

Smiling Macaria said, "Good for a minute there I thought you were losing your edge," then turned to join him at the car.

———

Segel realized immediately obtaining the files and removing Beck from the chess board was crucial, as the D.E.C.'s findings were surprisingly impressive to the right parties.

Almost three hours later Segel was in his rented estate in Harris Hill, NY, one of the richer suburbs north of Buffalo. He was rooted in his study still reading the downloaded information on his laptop, giving himself self-congratulations over his brilliance.

The man had been in his study since Macaria brought them home, reading and re-reading every line, result, and statistical fact the D.E.C. had discovered, almost committing the files to memory, and before he finished the report, Segel knew he had to make a deal with the Seneca Nation of Indians.

Sitting behind his two-hundred-year-old desk, rumored to have belonged to Thomas Jefferson, Regino watched as Macaria walk into the study, carrying a bottle of seventy-five-year-old cognac and two lead-crystal glasses. She placed the glasses on the desk, then poured some cognac into both, picked up her glass, then plopped herself into one of the high-backed, dark green leather chairs. Theirs was not the normal employer/employee relationship.

He looked up from the papers, took off his reading glasses, then said, "Making yourself at home again I see," then took a small swallow of the smooth, warm, spicy palate with a silky finish.

"You know me, I like to be comfortable," Macaria said as she twirled the stem of her glass in-between her slender finger. "Anything good in there, worth killing over?" she asked and gestured towards the files by nodding her head once.

"More than I'd hoped," Regino answered back. Seeing his sometime sexual partner's interest was piqued, he continued. "Have you ever heard of calcite?" Macaria shook her head, "I didn't think so", he said, then held up his hand. "Not to insult you my dear, but you're not a chemist or a geologist. Calcite's a crystalline mineral; it has been used in Ancient Egypt in carvings related to some of their goddesses. Nowadays it is used in soil remediation and stabilization and concreate repair."

"And this is of interest because...." Macaria trailed off.

"During the Second World War calcite was used in anti-aircraft guns and bombing sights, making it unbelievably valuable to the war effort, as much as paper or tin. Another aspect the government was interested in was experimenting with the mineral was an invisibility cloak." Regino saw his personal assistant stop twirling the glass in her fingers, because he captured her full attention. "Now I know you're aware of S.I.'s weapons division, we've contracts with the government," then stopped to correct himself, "Hold that thought; various governments, along with approximately half of our governmental clients, are not on speaking terms with the other half, and a few have, let's just say, some significant extremist views."

Regino got up to stretch his legs, arched his back, and rotated his shoulders till there was an audible pop. He had become stiff and achy from sitting still for so long.

Macaria patiently waited for him to continue, by taking a sip. Regino picked up his glass, inhaled deeply detecting apricot, vanilla, toasted nuts, and something that reminded him of old library books, took a good sip, then continued. "What you don't know is S.I.'s weapon's division is far more advanced than you can imagine. We've projects involving robotics, cybernetics, bioweapons, and I don't mean germ warfare. I am talking about genetic and cybernetic enhancements to humans, and that's on top of the battle armor weapons we've developed," then he shifted the direction of the conversation.

"Now imagine if you will, how much more dangerous United States forces would have been against the Axis if they'd had stealth technology back then. Several years back, our weapons' designers began looking at the old research from the past ninety years, and believe an invisibility cloak, is possible based on those old calcite studies."

"So, what does this all have to with the reports and the Indians?" Macaria asked."

After a prolonged sigh, Regino smiled and replied, "Last year, the D.E.C. conducted a routine geological and environmental study on the reservation to ensure all was well. They unearthed a colossal, underground vein of calcite. Owing to the recently deceased Mr. Beck, we are the sole possessors of this knowledge, and Segel International is keenly interested in negotiating with the Native community to acquire the land.

Macaria began stretching out in the chair like a lounging cat and said, "You think they'll sell?"

"As my uncle says, 'Everyone's got a price, you just gotta know what it is.' Besides, there's less than forty-five people living on the reservation. You honestly believe if they were offered enough, they wouldn't move and get the hell out of the area?"

Macaria thought for a moment, continuing to recline like a feline and said, "I don't know, maybe, I mean people do get attached to their homes."

He just looked at his aide, then said, "You didn't."

"No, but I've never been sentimental. Might explain why I blew up the family home before running away."

"Knew there was a reason I hired you on."

"So, when do you make the offer?"

"I've already got the accountants looking at the numbers, I should hear from them in less than twenty-four hours, after that I'll make the offer."

"I admit I'm a little shocked at all this," Macaria admitted, then took a big swallow of her drink.

"How so?"

"Well, not so much the calcite, I knew in dealing with Beck and the D.E.C. it was related to something in the ground, just not what. What surprises me is the potential for stealth technology and the weapons division is staggering. I had no idea the company was into cyber and bioweapons."

Regino showed a sly smile, which was barely perceivable, unless one looked right at him. "Just because we share a bed from time to time, doesn't mean I share all my secrets with you, my dear." Then he raised his glass to toast the moment, as Macaria did the same.

Regino sat back down as Macaria continued, "I know you were tied up with the files, and didn't want to be disturbed, but I knew you'd want to be notified. It's all over the news and the internet."

Regino saw a slight change in the beautiful bodyguard's flawless face, a look of disbelief and shock, which till now she hid well. "What happened?" he asked with his face changing into a question mark.

"In downtown Buffalo, a massive wave from Lake Erie and struck the Canalside area. There's no confirmed body count yet. Rescue and recovery teams are on the scene."

Regino turned around and faced the portrait of his late parents that hung behind his desk, and looked up at them, then smiled. "Really," was all he said.

"What are you thinking?" Macaria asked as she got up and poured herself a second cognac.

Turning sharply on his heels to look in her violet eyes, the industrialist said, "This could be an opportunity," then took the bottle from her and poured himself a second drink as well.

FOUR

Nick Wolfhart was home in his two-story log cabin, he had built by hand back in the late sixties, on the Cattaraugus Reservation, just over a half an hour away from Buffalo.

The eighty-plus-year-old, with long, silvery hair that reached down his back, wore a face etched with the lines of wisdom and experience, was in his upstairs office, having just finished double-checking his legal documents to ensure everything was in order, when noises from downstairs captured his attention.

Walking past various framed pictures of his late wife and daughter, which hung on the near wall, among others perched on shelves and bookcases, Wolfhart could hear his visitor rummaging in the kitchen, at the rear of the cabin. The refrigerator opened, bottles clinked around, then the fridge door closed with a slight thud. At the foot of the stairs Wolfhart clearly heard a bottlecap popping off, what he knew was one of his beer bottles, and from the sounds of his visitor's footsteps and breathing patterns, the full-blooded Senecan knew who was making himself at home.

As Wolfhart entered the kitchen, he remarked, "Helping yourself to my beer again?" while he headed to the refrigerator to grab a cold one for himself. After twisting off the cap, he sat down opposite the intruder at the central island, which was adorned with brown and tan tiles complementing the kitchen's decor.

With a gravelly voice tinged with an English accent, the bald-headed man shot back, "I figured one less wouldn't kill you. 'Sides you people aren't too great with fire water, right?" He took another swig from the bottle as he smiled. "Do me a favor and get some good English ale, this lite beer runs through me like a garden hose."

Wolfhart gave a half a shake of his head and smirked "And if you weren't already bald, you English prick, I'd scalp you." Wolfhart smiled back at Orsen Dorset. "So, you see him?"

"Yeah," Dorset said hesitantly, "But we might have a problem, Mate."

A new rush of concern rose as Wolfhart, and he placed his beer bottle on the island counter. "What happened Orsen?"

After a moment of an uncomfortable silence Dorset let out a long sigh and admitted one of the worse things a private investigator could when on a stake out, "Your grandson's good, I think he spotted me and knows he's being followed."

"Oh boy," was all Wolfhart said before he took a hard swallow, then said, "Tell me everything that happened."

Fifteen minutes later, the old friends were in Wolfhart's living room, at the front of the cabin, with Wolfhart sitting in his sturdy, solid, dark wooden chair that the man loved. Dorset was sitting back on the tan loveseat, up against the bay window, at the front of the house, reporting his surveillance over the last three days. Both men were nursing their second beers, as Wolfhart stayed quiet listening to everything being reported. "I know this is important stuff Nick, but shadowing Alex is a little much don't ya think?"

Wolfhart shook his head. "You don't understand why this is so important. You see, I have to know what kind of man he is."

"From what I've seen, he's no different than anyone else."

"No, he has to be better than most."

"What are you talking about? From what I've seen, he seems fine. He's good to his parents; he even moved back a few years ago after his father, ah..." Then Dorset double checked his memo book he pulled from his black jeans. "Here we go. His dad had experienced severe complications following pancreatic surgery. His recovery took much longer than anticipated. So, Alex returned to help his parents and manage their house. I can see why. It's a large property for a couple senior citizens to care for without any help. Remember, they're both 'bout five, six years older than you."

Wolfhart listened to Dorset finish his report. "He helps strangers when he's out, holds doors open for little old ladies and kids with their hands full, is a courteous driver, Alex even donates to a couple charities."

"It's not enough, I need to know everything I can, ASAP."

"I don't get it, what's so bloody important to seeing how good your grandson is before you meet him? I mean you expect him to help little old ladies across the street, rescue cats from trees, and pick up litter. Hell, he probably does all that and more."

Nick took a leap of faith, attempting to convince his best friend that the impossible was unfolding and the world required the extraordinary to happen. "Alright, I'll try to explain the whole thing, and I'm aware of how it may seem.

The story is as far-fetched to me as it might be to you. I was brought up by my grandparents, who instilled in me their beliefs, beliefs I once dismissed as bullshit. However, I've seen and experienced plenty mystical/paranormal incidents to be certain that what I'm about to share with you is the truth."

After taking another slug of beer, all Dorset said was, "Okay Nick, let's have."

Pausing to release his mounting frustration, Wolfhart with eyes, deep-set and thoughtful, reflected on a lifetime of stories and resilience, proceeded to recount the legends he had grown up with. "I am an actual descendant of Sagoye-watha, you know him as Red Jacket, but this story truly begins long before his birth, and starts with our brothers, the Lakota of the Plains, and their legend of the White Buffalo Calf Woman.

"Now Orsen," Wolfhart paused to take another sip, then rose and crossed the room to his old stone fireplace. The mantle was composed of three cedar logs, flanked by gray and gunmetal stones on either side. On top of the mantle were various personal mementos, a few framed photographs, and in the center was a small, wooden hand-made box. The age and weathering were clear. From inside the box Wolfhart pulled out what Orsen thought looked like a ribbon folded up on itself, but when he got a good look at the sacred item, the man from London's east end realized it was no ribbon.

Wolfhart opened it up fully, showing off family artifact in its entirety. Before Orsen could ask, Wolfhart answered his obvious question. "It's my family's Wampum Belt," he continued as he handed the belt to Orsen, who examined it like a crime scene investigator looking for fingerprints.

Then Wolfhart explained, "A wampum belt records histories and communicate ideas. Beaded patterns symbolize a person, a nation, or an event, among other things. They are made of clam shells, and the beads were handmade by breaking the shell, drilling a hole, then grinding it into a tubular shape. This one is a little different, several of the shells were dyed before the wampum was made."

The Wampum Belt was just over sixteen inches long, about the width of a ruler, and just by touch, one realized it was old, extremely old, so it was important to use a gentle touch. Some of the seashell pieces had been dyed in diverse colors; red, black, yellow, brown, blue, and green. Other pieces had been left white but yellowed with age. The pieces were arranged in a series of lines and patterns, with at the center of the belt being home to most of the blue and green pieces. They were in a circle-like pattern with the green pieces surrounded by the blue and white ones.

Wolfhart sat back down and continued, "This Wampum is very special; it's not an oral history of my family. No one is positive of its true age, but we know it pre-dates Red Jacket and Hiawatha, and tells a legend of the White Buffalo Calf Woman, of the Lakota Sioux.

"The legend of the White Buffalo Calf Woman dates back over six hundred years. The condensed version goes like this: two hunters encountered a beautiful maiden clad in white buckskin who materialized suddenly. Recognizing her as a Wakan, a holy entity, one hunter respectfully averted his gaze. The other, overcome with desire, sought to claim her. As he neared, the White Buffalo Calf Woman summoned him, and they were enveloped in a dust cloud. When it cleared, only a pile of bones remained beside her.

"She approached the respectful hunter and conveyed that she had granted another man's wish to experience a lifetime with her, but it occurred in a single moment, then he died. She instructed the hunter to inform his people to ready themselves for her coming, so she might show them the path. The White Buffalo Calf Woman then came to the village bearing a holy bundle and a prayer pipe, teaching the inhabitants the seven sacred methods of prayer. These prayers were meant for purification, child naming, healing ceremonies, adoption rituals, matrimonial unions, and the Vision Quest to communicate with the Creator.

Orsen asked, "All right Nick, but what does this all have to do with your family, I mean you're from a whole other group of Indians, right?"

Wolfhart nodded, feeling a little slighted because his friend was still using the terms to describe Indigenous Peoples, but at least Dorset didn't say redskins. "True, we're a different Nation," he said, raising his weathered hand to signal patience, "I'll get to that in a moment. After completing her teachings, the White Buffalo Calf Woman informed the Lakota that she would come back for the sacred bundle. She prophesied the coming of four ages, promising to observe the people at the end of each one, and vowed to return after the fourth age to bring harmony and spirituality back to a land in turmoil."

"She walked a short distance, glanced back at the people, and sat down. When she stood up, she had transformed into a black buffalo. The buffalo then lay down and stood again, this time as a yellow buffalo. The process was repeated, and she emerged as a red buffalo. Finally, after walking a bit further, she rolled on the ground and rose as a white buffalo calf, signifying the fulfillment of the White Buffalo Calf prophecy.

"See, Orsen the changing of the four colors, the Miracle represents the four colors of man—white, yellow, red, and black. These colors also represent the four directions, north, east, south, and west. The sacred bundle that was left to the Lakota people is still with them in a sacred place on the Cheyenne River Indian reservation in South Dakota."

"All right," Orsen said.

Wolfhart saw how totally fixated Orsen was on his story, finally beginning to understand more than he did before.

"In 1994, an extremely rare white albino buffalo calf was born in Wisconsin. Her owners named her Miracle. To the Lakota and a great many others, including non-Natives, Miracle represented the fulfillment of an ancient prophecy. Shortly after, the farm became a religious shrine, attracting hundreds of visitors worldwide. Now according to the prophecy, Miracle would change color five times, akin to the White Buffalo Calf Woman. The legend's most crucial aspect predicts at least five years of natural and human-induced disasters, such as fires, floods, earthquakes, typhoons, pollution, and wars, signifying the planet's self-healing process.

"Generations ago, my family's legacy began when an ancestor was commanded by a Wakan known as Ghost Walker, who wielded immense power. She decreed that our bloodline would serve as guardians to safeguard humanity's future. This wampum belt, bestowed by Ghost Walker, was to be handed down through generations until the prophesied time when a descendant of both the red man and the white would emerge."

From the expression on Orsen's face, Wolfhart saw he'd caught onto the stories, even though they were legends there was something to all of this. He knew superhumans existed in the world and some had gone back decades, even generations.

Orson said, "As a teenager in London, I witnessed a battle by Parliament Building where the London Underground, Anarchy, Jack B. Nimble, the Hood, and Sherwood held off an attack by the Queen of Harts and her *Alice in Wonderland* themed Red Guard. I'd seen superhumans in the news, the idea that one of my best friends might be a metahuman is something completely different, especially since you never showed any superhuman abilities when we spent time together in military operations.

"So, what can you do? Fly? Are invulnerable? Have super speed?"

Wolfhart saw Dorset's skepticism, so he stood up, reached into his black and white flannel shirt, and pulled out a metal arrowhead that hung around his neck. "This is the key, it unlocks the powers in my bloodline," he began explaining, and handed it to Orsen. It was a piece of metal formed into an arrowhead, with a howling wolf head, forged on the surface.

As he handed the necklace over, Wolfhart said, "I can't fly, but I can run as fast as a cougar, see as well as the eagle, have the senses of the wolf, and possess the strength of the bear."

Orsen began smirking. After catching his breath, the former SAS operative said, "Sorry, mate, I'm not trying to insult you, but it's all hard to believe. Look at it from my point of view."

Instinctively, Wolfhart clutched his family heirloom, shut his eyes, and felt a surge coursing through his veins. A blue-whitish aura, reminiscent of lightning, surrounded him. When he opened his eyes, they had changed shape, resembling those of a bird of prey, with the whites almost black. Wolfhart's breathing rapidly increased, and his body seemed to firm up and gain muscle. Orsen's smirk vanished.

FIVE

To say Marie felt jumbled and confounded would be like saying a tornado is a bit breezy. Her thoughts were a whirlwind of confusion, leaving her utterly disoriented. She found herself headed towards a nearby parking lot that had been transformed by the authorities in record time. The emergency weather alerts had warned city officials and the necessary parties.

Marie was not alone walking the half mile; she was joined by her co-workers and people from the surrounding businesses. All the workers and visitors around Canalside were headed to one of the two camps set up in the downtown area.

At first, it seemed like Marie might have been recovering from an overnight Vegas-style bachelorette party, she was shell-shocked, and as she followed the procession of people, everything came back to her.

She had no memory of hitting her head during the panic in the conference room, but a throbbing pain on the right side of her head told Marie something happened. Instinctively, she reached up and felt a slight bump quickly forming. When she touched it with her right index and middle fingers, a sharp pain jolted through her head. "Ow, damnit," she yelled aloud to no one in particular, already knowing she'd have a decent-sized bulge on her forehead in a day or two, then everything came back to her.

———

Marie, like everyone else, leapt up from her chair once she saw the seiche rolling in towards them. Two managers who sat nearby came out of their seats, flying into a complete panic and barged past everyone. One of them shoved Marie aside, causing her to stumble. As she attempted to regain her footing, Marie collided with the conference table. A surge of pain shot through her head as she struck the edge. Groggy, she felt a pulsing sensation begin to swell on the right side of her forehead. The surrounding turmoil became a blur as she sought stability, the sounds of frantic voices and rapid footsteps merging into a faint buzz. An associate, whom she didn't know personally, but recognized from the Niagara Falls, N.Y. office, helped her to her feet. She didn't even feel the jolt of the seventy-plus foot seiche that passed by the office, as if it were a speeding car zooming past an unnoticed animal on the side of the road.

After the wave passed by and headed further north, Marie looked out through the floor-to-ceiling windows and saw white caps everywhere. Smaller waves crested and ran ashore all along the shoreline. The lake churned up a lot of debris, wreckage, rubbish, clumps of seaweed, and waste, all rising to the surface.

Once things calmed down, Marie and the rest of the staff were ordered outside by the office manager, Jeremy. "Everyone needs to leave the building and head to the parking lot! The building might not be stable after the impact! If anyone needs medical help, we'll call 911 from outside. Grab your things and go!" Marie packed up her laptop and files as Jeremy ordered two of his assistants to help get everyone outside. "Chuck, Terra, help me clear the rest of the building and make sure everyone clears out."

Marie then followed the staff into the parking lot, where she saw employees and customers from the adjacent restaurant and the Buffalo Heritage Carousel already calling 911. Emergency services were already mobilized thanks to the advanced warnings. Within moments of coming outside, Marie and everyone there heard police, fire, and EMT sirens wailing throughout downtown, coming rapidly towards them.

While Marie examined her head in a sideview mirror of her car, two white and blue BPD squad cars and a police SUV arrived as a light rain began to fall over the area, adding to the surreal atmosphere of the chaotic scene.

Four officers got out of the vehicles and began looking over the victims. Three officers checked on the people who looked the worst, but no one was injured: no bleeding, broken bones, or mass hysteria. Some, like Marie, had some bumps and bruises, and most everyone was shell-shocked to some extent.

Watching things play out Marie realized there were those who might have some form of trauma because they were walking around in various stupors. One woman, she knew from the Northtowns office collapsed on the blacktop and balled herself up and was rocking back and forth against the building.

Marie went over and scrunched down to see if she could help. "Hey, it's Pattie, right" she asked. The older, heavyset, ash-blonde woman almost seemed catatonic, not even looking at Marie, until she asked, "I was wondering if you know what time it is? I think my watch stopped."

Finally, Pattie stopped rocking, glanced at her slender, gold wristwatch and said, "It's twenty after five."

"Thanks," Marie answered back, then asked, "do you want to leave?" and offered her hand to help pull Pattie up.

As Marie helped Pattie, the fourth officer who arrived in the SUV immediately got on his radio and requested more EMTs to be sent to their location. He then switched the radio over to the P.A. setting. "Attention everyone, medical personnel are on their way here. If you need assistance, let one of the officers know and we'll get help to you as soon as possible." That captured everyone's attention. The burly, African American supervisor continued, "We need the area evacuated immediately. If you're able to, make your way to the Red Cross emergency camp that's being set up in the parking lot between Baltimore and Mississippi. From there you can make further arrangements to be picked up or take one of the Metro Buses that will be provided by the NFTA."

Marie walked over to the closest officer to her, a young, blonde female, who was about her age and was about to ask why she couldn't drive her car, when several co-workers began yelling out the same questions, but they were more vocal about it than Marie was.

As a pair of ambulances rolled up, the supervisor continued, "For your safety, the area needs to be evacuated immediately. Until the buildings along the waterfront are deemed structurally safe, no one can re-enter any building, but you need to leave your vehicles where they are." There was a lot of pushback from people who demanded to take their cars out, but the officers stood firm since they were under orders.

"Right now, we cannot allow that because no one knows what all the vibrations from these vehicles may do to the foundations of the buildings or the supports for the Skyway. City Engineers or the Army Corps of Engineers will be examining the structures as soon as possible." The explanation seemed to satisfy most, but not all.

Marie just stood there, her mind drifted back to when she lost her parents. For the second time in her life, Marie felt the same level of shock. She recalled her parents in the wreckage of their car, mangled with another vehicle, a burning hulk on the side of a California highway. She remembered just sitting on the blacktop until the California Highway Patrol showed up and helped her, much like the first responders were doing now.

The howl from a third approaching ambulance snapped Marie back to reality and the blonde officer showed her concern. "Are you all right ma'am? Do you want someone to look at your head?" she asked noticing the knot starting to show some discoloration.

"Ah, no, I think I'm going to be all right," Marie was able to stammer out. "What was that the other officer said about the Red Cross?"

It was then the blonde asked, "Are you sure you're going to be alright?"

Instinctively Marie touched the bump, again and with a touch of more steadiness in her voice Marie said "Yes, it's just a slight knock I took."

"Well, if you're sure," the rookie said hesitantly. "The Red Cross is setting up a base camp where folks can get help if they need it. Just go straight down South Park," she said while pointing in the direction of the base camp. "Past the arena, they are setting up in the parking lot on the next block. Follow the others, you cannot miss it," she added pointing in the direction of a line of the evacuees headed towards the camp. "Now are you going to be okay to walk down there?" the officer asked one final time.

The women turned their heads when they heard an authoritative voice say, "I'll make sure she gets down there okay," and saw Jeremey stepping up and taking responsibility for Marie, which surprised her, but the gesture made her smile.

———

Ten minutes later Marie and Jeremy made their way through the misting rain, which was letting up. They were in the middle of the procession that went past the Cobblestone Bar & Grille and crossed Mississippi Street, where the Red Cross and what looked like an invading force of first responders and volunteers had set up their site. People were coming in from all over the Canalside area, swarming like a horde of ants going after an ice cream cone left on the ground.

The walk was quiet and surreal. The crowd was subdued, almost shell-shocked, unlike the usual post-game hustle. Marie heard the occasional disgruntled comments that floated around about not being allowed to drive their cars and wondering where the local heroes were—Republic Steele, the Norseman, the Garda team, or even semi-retired ones like Skyway and Lady Liberty. Not a single sighting of any of them.

"You gonna be okay?" Jeremey asked as they reached the parking lot.

"Yes, I'll be fine," Marie answered. "Thanks for your concern," grateful for his watchful eye, because it seemed as if the female officer wasn't going to let her go without Jermey's help.

As they looked around, they were surprised at how quickly things were mobilized. The parking lot held five tents, twenty by twenty feet, arranged in a straight line. Victims stood in lines, registering so the authorities could have an accurate head count and knew not to look for them among the injured, missing, or dead. Across the parking lot were another four large tents with volunteers offering coffee, juice, small snacks, and even a kind word to help people feel human again. Folding tables and chairs had been set up throughout the parking lot, allowing people to reach out to family or friends, letting them know they were alive and arrange to be picked up.

After registering, Marie and Jeremy eventually collapsed at one of the tables, where what looked like exhausted survivors were recovering. Jeremy then offered, "You want some coffee or something?" He looked like he could barely drag himself out of his chair. Marie thought his usually polished appearance was replaced by someone who looked fifty years older. Jeremy's tan skin seemed pale and ashen, and his dark hair, usually neatly combed, was tousled and scruffy. Marie then wondered how she must look after this afternoon.

"No thank you," Marie said looking just as deflated as everyone else who came staggering in. "Actually, I'm not much of a coffee drinker, I think I just want to get home and get some rest."

"Can't blame you," he said as he reached inside his sports jacket for his cell, while Marie began going through her laptop bag.

"Damnit," Marie uncharacteristically yelled aloud in a panic, then she stood up beginning to search her pockets.

"What's wrong," Jeremey asked looking up at Marie, who was moving in a frenzied fury.

"My cell, I can't find it," she practically yelled out for everyone to hear. A couple of people glanced in her direction, but most just ignored her.

"Take it easy," Jeremey said as he got up and placed his hands on her shoulders, trying to calm her down. He was afraid getting upset after the blow she took wouldn't be good for her. "Now are you sure it's not in your bag?"

"No, it's not here." Marie emptied her bag onto the table. After examining everything it hit Marie, "Damnit, I must have left it in my car. I know I had it with me when I left my office, because I put it in the cup holder, and checked for client updates from Midge."

"Okay good, at least you know it's safe," Jeremey said seeing Marie was calming down. "The police said they'd be keeping an eye on the parking lots and our cars. You can use my cell to call for a ride. Where are you headed?" he said handing his phone to her.

"West Seneca, I don't live that far from my office."

"Oh okay," he sheepishly said. "I've got to call my wife for a pickup, but we live in North Tonawanda…"

Seeing what he was leading to Marie held up her hand interrupting him, "Right, we're in opposite directions, I appreciate the thought, but calling for a ride should be fine. Call your wife first and let her know you are all right. I still have to figure out who I'm going to call."

"What about taking one of the buses?" Jeremey asked as he began dialing.

"I really don't feel like taking one, especially after banging my head, then having to walk from wherever in West Seneca to my cottage, especially since I'm not sure where they'll be dropping people off."

"Yeah, you're right," he said as he sat down, then called his wife. As they talked, Marie began packing up her case, trying to figure out who to call for her ride.

As Marie considered her options, she was among the first to notice the air surrounding the downtown area grew silent. No sirens, no traffic sounds, no aircraft flying overhead, just unnerving dead stillness.

Marie, who possessed a sixth sense, realized the atmosphere had become charged with nervous energy. Everyone suddenly stopped whatever they were doing and turned their heads, looking in a southeasterly direction, as a low, booming echo came from above.

At first, Marie, like everyone else, thought it was a jet plane or some other low-flying aircraft. However, they quickly realized that whatever was approaching was too low to the ground. The echo grew louder, and people became frantic, panicking and beginning to run or look for shelter. Three men and two women shoved their way towards a nearby van, assaulting the driver and taking his keys before piling in. They then tore a doughnut on the side street, nearly sideswiping a police car and an ambulance. When the rumble came overhead, Marie and the crowd felt a renewed sense of hope.

A two-tone green glow illuminated a portion of the darkening, gray skies. A lighter shade of neon green surrounded a darker, deeper forest green. The glow streaked in like a shooting star, at the center were four figures inside the energy field. Everyone on site recognized who was coming to help and the fear and tension seemed to vanish, at least for a moment because The Garda had arrived.

Maria had read about the Garda online when she moved to Buffalo. According to the metahuman chat boards, some believe the group has existed since South Buffalo's formation in the 1850s. Rumors claim St. Patrick blessed four citizens to protect the Irish residents. The current team was led by Samhain, a Celtic priest whose face hidden by a dark cloak and hood, wielding a mystic lantern granting him various powers, including transporting his teammates: Fortune, who can manipulate probability; Banshee, a wraith with sonic vocal powers, rumored to be the spirit from Irish folklore; and Red Hand, a hero from Northern Ireland with an armored suit containing his energy form, granting him superhuman abilities.

Marie and Jeremey, like everyone else, watched in

amazement, with a renewed sense of relief and hope, as the energy field hovered above the parking lot, then a stream of green, flaming energy came from Samhain's lantern onto the escaping van. Once the ray of light reached the four-ton battering ram, it enveloped the vehicle, which froze in place. A moment later the van, surrounded by emerald flames, rose off the ground, hovered for a moment, then floated back to the parking lot. Once back on the blacktop, police officers took the group into custody.

After things settled, Samhain gave his orders loud enough for everyone to hear. His voice cut through the air with an urgency that demanded immediate attention from everyone within earshot. "Fortune, coordinate with the authorities below, join us when you can. Red Hand scan along the waterfront for survivors who may be in need and the buildings for structural damage. Banshee, you, and I will synchronize with our Canadian allies, and see where we can be of aid."

When Marie looked up at the heroes, she locked eyes with Samhain. Time stood still as their gazes met. His piercing green eyes, partially hidden by his hood, glowed with the same eerie energy as his lantern did, casting shadows across his rugged, red-bearded face. Marie felt a surge of emotions, fear, curiosity, and a strange familiarity. The Celtic knotwork on Samhain's cloak seemed to pulse with life, responding to their silent exchange. His presence was overwhelming, a blend of ancient power and enigmatic charm that both intrigued and unsettled her. In that moment, she sensed the weight of centuries in his gaze, as if he could see into her very soul. The lantern's glow intensified, hinting at its immense power and the secrets it guarded.

Without saying another word, the mystic opened his energy field, extending a ramp of glowing, fiery energy to the parking lot, allowing Fortune to ride her custom emerald and black racing motorcycle down to the blacktop. At the same time, Red Hand and Banshee went airborne, he with his jet thrusters releasing energy bursts, and she with her sonic cries, everyone in the area felt in their cores. Once Fortune was on the ground, the Celtic pilgrim followed his teammates towards the waterfront, his lantern lighting the way.

Marie's attention was split, like everyone else's, between watching the trio fly off and Fortune stick her landing. Once on the blacktop, she hopped off her cycle, then began speaking with the authorities as ordered.

A throng began swarming around the redheaded heroine, clad in her three-tone green and gold trimmed costume, either for a look, or to ask where the Garda had been, but several officers were able to keep the crowd away, so she could speak to the officials in privacy.

Once order was restored, Marie thought about who she could call. *Maybe Midge,* then she realized she couldn't call Midge or any of her co-workers or neighbors. Marie silently cursed herself because, like most people who rely too heavily on their smartphones, all her contacts were in the phone, and she never bothered to memorize any numbers.

Marie watched as Jeremy reassured his wife that he was perfectly fine but needed to be picked up.

"Yeah, Terri, I promise I'm fine," she heard him say, then she looked down at her laptop sitting on the table. In that moment, she had a flash of inspiration. She opened her work laptop and then her client files.

As Marie began logging in, Jeremy finished speaking with his wife. "Man, that's something. Never saw The Garda in person before and I've lived here my whole life."

"Me either, but when I was still in California, I saw some of the Blockbusters fight those sports fanatics, the M.V.P.s, at

Sea World. And my mother was saved by Decathlon back at the '84 Olympics."

"So," Jeremy asked as he retook his seat and handed over his phone, "Jessie and I will give you a lift home if you can't reach anyone. Know who you're calling?"

Marie smiled slightly and gave a wince of a nod, "Yeah, I just hope he's available."

SIX

For almost two hours, Alex was riveted by the live local news. However, after forty-five minutes of coverage, he realized the anchors, reporters, and weatherpersons were repeating themselves. Despite watching all that time, he remained hypnotized by the footage until he finally realized how numb he felt from the shock.

Officials at the National Weather Service reported the seiche started around 1:30 PM, originating on the Buffalo side of Lake Erie. It generated enough energy to reach the shores of Sandusky, Ohio, before boomeranging back towards Western New York. The seiche reached an unprecedented size, with an estimated height of nearly seven stories and a width of around four-hundred and fifty yards. Nothing like this had been seen on the lake before.

The seiche surged past Tift Nature Preserve and Wilkerson Point, barreling through the Canalside area before continuing its destructive path north towards the Peace Bridge and Unity Island. The surging waters struck the smaller islands lining the Buffalo and Niagara Rivers. The wave's rampage finally ended when it slammed ashore at East River Road, near the South Grand Island Bridge.

Video footage of the seiche came from several sources, including the Seneca One Tower, which captured the seiche making its way into the downtown corridor. Various cameras on downtown rooftops, traffic cameras along the 290, and smart-phone recordings from both sides of the U.S./Canadian border provided comprehensive views of the seiche's impact.

At this point, the body count and financial toll remain unknown, but questions were already being asked, and fingers were being pointed.

When Alex heard his parents pull into the driveway, he snapped out of his mesmerized state. They entered through the front door, situated in the center of the ranch-style home. Alex turned off the television, left his half of the house next to the two-car garage, walked through his in-law suite, and joined his mother in the sunken living room.

He sat down on the blue loveseat against the wall dividing the living room from the dining area, kitchen, and the master and guest bedrooms. The news was already on the wall-mounted flat screen to Alex's right, and for the next few minutes, the only sound came from the television.

Finally, Celeste, a white-haired librarian, turned to Alex during a commercial break and asked, "Did you hear what happened?"

"Yeah, I did," he said, still feeling shell-shocked. Without taking his gaze off the screen, Alex asked, "Where's Dad?"

"He's changing. By the way, the cousins said to say 'Hi.'" Then as if on cue, Reggie entered, having changed from his formal clothes into sweatpants, sneakers, and a retro Buffalo Braves T-shirt. Carrying the matching sweat jacket, he sat in his recliner opposite Celeste's matching chair at the far end of the living room, facing the television.

The Harlows continued watching the local news, which aired uninterrupted, encroaching on the NBC World News slot. Eventually, the local anchor paused, glanced off-camera as if listening to someone, then turned back to the viewers. "All right, I've just been told we're going to take a brief commercial break for station identification, but we'll resume our team coverage when we return."

"Thank God none of us were downtown today," Celeste finally said without taking her gray eyes off the screen. An ad for an upcoming Pre-Thanksgiving sale at a local mattress dealership was playing to no one specific, as she continued wringing her hands, a habit she had whenever her anxiety spiked.

With his eyes still locked on the screen Alex vaguely said, "Tell me about it, and I thought what I heard was big news."

"What are you talking about?" Reggie asked, turning towards Alex.

Unsure of how to tell his parents, Alex decided to go for it. "You remember how I reached out to Homeward Angels back in late January, or early February? Well, I heard from my case worker, Marie, this afternoon, and she said the state is finally releasing copies of my files. Marie will call me with a time to check over everything once they're delivered."

Thrilled for Alex, Celeste nearly shouted, "Alex that's fantastic! We know you've wanted this for a long time!" Since the Harlows had explained his adoption to him at age five, Alex had harbored countless questions. Now, as he sought answers for himself, he also tried to address all the questions his parents had.

"So did your case manager have any information for you?" his dad asked as he slipped his reading glasses on.

Alex shook his head. "No, Marie doesn't have any info, yet" he said reminded Reggie of what he'd just said.

Celeste asked, "So how do you feel? I mean, are you excited, nervous?" The look in her fatigued, gray eyes told Alex she was happy for him, but he knew her concerns were enduring. Alex sensed that, for longer than his dad realized, his mom's perspective was that he'd been given up by his biological family and there was no telling what might happen if he met them. Alex suspected she hoped he had no desire to get together with them. To be honest Alex wasn't positive about how he felt.

"Well, yeah, I think I'm feeling both, I guess. I mean when Marie told me, it was like POW right there in my face, kinda like a flashbulb going off, blinding me. But I've had some time to let it sink in and think about it, sort of, I mean with all this," then Alex gestured towards the television.

Alex went on to tell his parents everything about his conversation with Marie, as the news coverage continued, and their conversation offered a needed return to normalcy.

Finally, Reggie mentioned the five-hundred-pound gorilla hanging from the ceiling down. "So what are you planning to do? I mean are you going to meet your family?"

The question struck Alex like a cold wave crashing over him at the beach, even though he had anticipated it. The topic had always seemed so distant, something he only occasionally pondered and imagined, but never truly considered as a real possibility.

His head lowered slightly as he glanced at the dark, deep living room carpeting. "Hmm, to be honest, I don't know." He looked his parents in the eye, trying to make eye contact with both simultaneously, careful not to appear rude. "I've never really considered the possibility, so I guess I'll take things slowly and review everything as it comes in. Maybe Marie has some ideas; after all, this is her area of expertise."

As they continued their conversation and Celeste told Alex about the monthly luncheon with their cousins, the phone rang. Reggie,, being the closest, picked up the cordless handset in the living room and answered, "Hello," while Celeste muted the TV.

"Just a moment, please." Reggie looked to Alex and extended the phone. "It's for you."

"Hello?"

"Alex, it's Marie. I hate to ask to ask this, but I need a favor."

SEVEN

Normally, a drive downtown would take Alex about twenty minutes, but tonight it took over fifty minutes due to the unusually heavy traffic heading in and out of the area. The congestion reminded Alex of the traffic after a Bills or Sabers' game, or when the Erie County Fair is in town.

Once Alex reached 'The Valley,' one of the original Irish neighborhoods in the Queen City, the drive slowed to a crawl.

When the gunmetal gray/blue Charger reached Chicago Street, Alex encountered a police detour. A white and blue cruiser was parked diagonally at the intersection, with its red, white, and blue lights flashing, causing Alex to squint as he approached. It was reminiscent of entering a car wash. The officers allowed one car through at a time after checking in with the drivers, much like the border crossings at the Peace or Rainbow Bridges.

An all-American-looking officer leaned into Alex's window. "What's your purpose for coming down here?" he asked.

Alex thought the policeman looked like an action figure

come to life, with blue eyes, perfect blonde hair, and white-capped teeth. Even from behind the steering wheel, Alex could tell this guy was a bruiser. "I'm picking up a friend who was working downtown today. She was told she had to leave her car, her office is almost under the Skyway," he answered, trying to remember everything Marie had told him.

"You know where you're headed?"

"Yeah, she's at the Red Cross camp, near the arena."

"All right," the officer said, standing up straight, pointing the direction Alex needed to take. What you're gonna do is go down Chicago for two blocks, make a left, then head to Baltimore Street and make another left. Basically, just follow the line of cars." Alex glanced in the direction the officer indicated. "That's where the camp is, in that parking lot. We blocked off several streets, making them one-way for traffic control. After you find your friend, head back towards South Park, and that'll take you away from downtown."

"Got it, thanks," Alex said, and he followed the line of cars, feeling like he was in the world's longest drive-thru.

About ten minutes later, Alex finally reached Baltimore and scanned the grounds for Marie. It was tricky, with the constant stop-and-go traffic, pedestrians crossing without looking, and a rusted-out pickup right ahead of him. Finally, about halfway down the block, Alex spotted Marie waving, clutching her laptop bag, accompanied by a man he didn't know. "All right, here we are," he said to himself.

Amazingly, a car pulled away from the curb, freeing up a spot for Alex. He saw Marie clearly thanking her escort. Watching them shake hands, Alex felt a twinge of jealousy but couldn't quite figure out why. With his window still down, he overheard her say, "I will."

Normally, Alex would have gotten out to open the door

for her, but the heavy traffic made it impossible. She opened the passenger door and got in. As he slowly pulled away from the curb, Marie closed the door and caught her breath. "I really appreciate this, Alex," she said. Tossing her bag into the back seat, she added, "Jeremy offered to drive me home if I couldn't get a ride."

"Really," Alex said with a quizzical look, his left eyebrow rising, Spock-like.

Marie quickly explained, feeling an uncommon moment of embarrassment. "Jeremy manages the downtown office, and his wife is picking him up. He offered to drive me home, but they live in the Northtowns, and you were a lot closer."

"And with this traffic, no telling how long it'll take her," he continued. "No problem, kid. I'm glad you're all right. But you never told me what you were doing down here when you called."

"There was a managers' meeting downtown. After things settled down, I discovered I'd left my phone in my car, and all my contacts are in my phone. But I had my work laptop with me, which has my client records."

Figuring out the rest, Alex jumped in. "So, you looked up my number and called. Smart."

Alex watched as Marie closed her ice-blue eyes and rested her head on her right fist against the passenger window, finally allowing herself to relax. He had more questions, but figured now wasn't the time and decided to let Marie share at her own pace. "So, when are you getting your car back?"

"The police said nobody can go back to the area until city engineers can examine it to ensure it's safe. They said an official announcement would be made soon, but didn't give a timeframe. There are concerns regarding the wave may have shaken the foundation of the buildings and the Skyway supports."

Alex let out a soft whistle. "Yeah, I can see why they'd want to make sure it was safe."

As they passed the Tesla Plant, Alex noticed Marie was staring at him, and he got the feeling she trusted him "So, what happened with the bump?" he asked as they turned from South Park to Seneca Street, leading right to Marie's neighborhood.

"Oh, that's nothing really," Marie said, gingerly touching the knot on her forehead. Then she flipped down the passenger visor to check her reflection in the vanity mirror. "Damn," she muttered, noticing the bruise forming. As they entered West Seneca, Marie recounted what happened in the conference room. "I don't know those two guys. I guess they work out of the downtown office."

"And Jeremy didn't mention them while you were waiting?" Alex asked, his anger rising as he gripped the steering wheel so hard, he felt and heard his knuckles crack without any effort.

"No, to be honest, I think they're the last thing on his mind."

"Yeah, that's understandable," Alex said, silently hoping someday he'd meet them.

As they made their way through the heart of West Seneca, Alex realized the traffic was abnormally light, and figured people either were holding up with their families or downtown, the way he was, then asked, "Want me to stop somewhere and get you something to eat?"

They passed by several options—from fast food places, to gas station convenience stores, and long-established, popular restaurants.

"Thanks, but I just want to get home as I have dinner

waiting for me. I cook a lot over the weekends, then freeze portions, so when I get home, I can reheat."

Alex nodded. "Like I said, smart," he said, smiling at her as they pulled up to her house.

Marie rented a small, two-story, white and blue 1940s cottage off Mill Road, directly across from Queen of Heaven School.

Alex pulled into the driveway, which could easily hold six cars. The cottage had a two-car garage at the rear of the property, likely an addition, just like the brick chimney, he thought. It was surrounded by three similar houses that fit the heart of the West Seneca neighborhood, and Alex realized the place suited Marie.

"Nice-looking place," he said as he shut off the engine.

"Certainly is," Marie replied, digging in her bag for her keys. "I like the neighborhood, nice and peaceful mostly, except when the kids are getting out of school. Plus, it's a short walk to work if I feel like it, which I suspect will be the case for the next week at least. That's one major advantage of being within walking distance of the office."

"Right. Speaking of which, when you get word about your car, let me know and I'll drive you back downtown."

"Thank you, but I'm sure one of my girlfriends can drive me. I don't want to trouble you."

"No trouble. So, if they can't take you, just call me."

"I'll keep your offer in mind," Marie answered. Then they both grew quiet. Marie stared into his dark eyes and continued. "Again, I really appreciate this. Would you like to come in for a drink? I figure it's the least I owe you."

A small smile broke out, and Alex gave a semi shake of his head. "Ah, I'll take a rain check. I gotta get back home. Besides, I'm sure you want to get some rest after you eat, right?"

Marie smiled back, blushed a little, and nodded. "You are not far off from the truth; a rain check it is."

They sat there for a moment in a comfortable silence. "I have to go. I'll call you about that ride, okay."

"Right. You have a good night."

"You too, and thanks again."

Alex started the engine, but made sure Marie got inside safely. When she looked back over her shoulder, she gave a final wave, and he returned it. Once she was inside, Alex headed home. As intriguing as he found Marie, his thoughts returned to his biological family and the potential implications of this discovery.

EIGHT

Wolfhart sat in an Adirondack chair in his backyard, watching the sun set. It was mid-October, and the nights were arriving sooner. The air was getting chillier, with a nip that signaled winter's approach. Some mornings, frost covered lawns and vehicles, and to Wolfhart it seemed the cold and snow came earlier each year. The remains of dusky purple daylight were still visible as the colors shifted from shades of blue to purples and violets, eventually fading to black.

The nearly ninety-year-old Senecan contemplated the crackling fire in his fire pit: a ring of steel, surrounded by gray stones, topped by a large, triangular piece of stone set askew. A pleasant, sweet aroma from the maple and birch wood filled the night air. As Wolfhart watched the smoke rise and vanish into the sky, he felt like the oldest man alive.

He hated feeling drained most of the time—physically, mentally, and spiritually. He hated not knowing where his daughter was, let alone if she was still alive. Worst of all he hated thinking about Alex.

To be precise, hate wasn't accurate—it was jealousy.

Wolfhart envied his grandson's youth and strength. Alex's true journey was about to begin. He resented that Alex would be granted power from Grandmother Earth; command over fire, water, earth, and air. Only the Gods knew what other abilities Alex would receive. Though Wolfhart loved his animal-based powers, he craved first-hand knowledge of what Alex would experience.

Wolfhart sat there, nursing his fourth beer, wallowing in self-pity. The clouds slowly moved in, swallowing the stars. A rumble of thunder echoed forever, and startled, the bottle slipped from his grip. "Damnit." He picked up his beer from the grass. It had dropped straight down without spilling a drop.

As Wolfhart was about to take another swallow, a flash of lightning illuminated the skies behind the clouds. Suddenly, the fire roared to life with renewed ferocity, as if a drum of gasoline had been poured into it. A smoke column rose high above the cabin and the nearby pines and firs, reaching a massive size. Wolfhart knew what was happening.

The man was enveloped by a massive plume of dark smoke and couldn't see two feet in front of him, but Wolfhart knew who was responsible when he heard an elderly woman's voice he recognized materialize from the smoke.

"How goes your journey, my son? Something troubles you; I can feel it."

An elderly Native American medicine woman emerged from the darkness. Her gray braided hair ran all the way down her back. She was dressed in a traditional long over-dress, the color of faded rose. Below, it was black, along with her leggings and moccasins. Around her neck was a neck-lace composed of animal sinew, polished animal bones, and gleaming rocks. On her right wrist, she wore a tarnished silver bracelet with a green gem set in the center. On the left, she wore strips of animal hide woven into a thin bracelet with a blue gem.

The medicine woman, only known as Grandmother, stopped advancing and sat down cross-legged in front of Wolfhart. She carried a smoldering wand of sage in her right hand, fanning it back and forth. The sickly sweet, dark green and gray smoke originated from the wand.

Wolfhart told Grandmother of his frustration. "It's stupid to be jealous of Alex, but still…."

Grandmother held up her left hand. "You are only human, my son, but these feelings will pass. You are not the only member of your lineage to have felt this way. Almost everyone who has worn the arrowhead and borne your family's responsibility has hoped to be the one."

Grandmother sat in silence, and so did Wolfhart, consumed by shame. After a moment of uncomfortable quiet, Grandmother spoke. "I sense something else troubles you."

Wolfhart admitted his deeper concern. "You're right, but I can't explain. I feel something's coming around the bend and can't get out of the way. I'm afraid I won't have the time I need to explain everything to Alex."

"When you say 'everything'?" Grandmother asked.

"About the calling, our family history," Wolfhart paused, looking away from Grandmother. He could only support his head in his left hand, his arm leaning on his chair's armrest, then finally he admitted the worst part. "And about his mother. How do I tell my grandson I drove away his mother, my only child away? I've no idea where she is, or if she's alive."

He looked for an answer from Grandmother, then realized he was alone. He knew Grandmother had spoken enough this night. With no warning, she'd ended their conversation. This wasn't the first time, and he never liked it, but he had no choice. It was her way of telling him, "You'll do the right thing when the time comes." He'd known Grandmother almost his whole life. Though she'd been elderly when he was a boy, something amazed Wolfhart more than her mystical powers: the woman was never wrong. Somehow, she always knew.

Dread still ran like a chill through his core. The clouds and smoke departed, the fire was extinguished, and the beer was empty. Wolfhart considered opening another bottle but decided against it. Orson was picking him up early in the morning and he needed a clear head. Walking to the cabin, he began to pray his feelings were wrong. Except for the planet's preservation, what Wolfhart wanted most was the opportunity to meet and get to know his grandson.

What kind of man was Alex?

NINE

A few miles away, somewhere alongside the Cattaraugus Creek, in the woods between the towns of Irving and Versailles stood a longhouse most people were unaware of. The traditional dwelling for members of the Iroquois nation was long and narrow, about a hundred meters long by seven meters wide. It was made of elm and oak, covered in animal skins. A stranger passing by might think it was a historic site, in reality the longhouse was Grandmother's home, where she had lived with the land for a very long time, though no one knew exactly how long.

Among Grandmother's abilities is astral projection, what some call an out-of-body experience, where she sends her astral body into a spiritual plane and/or the physical realm as a disembodied spirit. When her spirit returned to her body, Grandmother opened her eyes and the first thing she saw was her wolf companion, keeping watch next to her, in front of the fire ring made of several large stones near her longhouse, surrounded by four log benches. Once recovered, the elder breathed deeply, then reached inside her overdress and pulled out a small, aged, worn, and cracked leather pouch. She opened it, poured a sparkling blue powder into her wrinkled hand, and gently blew the powder into the fire.

The blazing oranges, glowing reds, and flickering yellows instantly turned to bluish-violet flames, growing in strength. The column of smoke became a lighter shade of lilac or mauve and rose with the swiftness of a falcon in the dive. Grandmother closed her seasoned eyes, still gleaming with untold stories, then breathed in deeply. The smoke had an aroma of sage, oak wood, spices, and fruits.

The Medicine Woman could now speak with The Sacred Circle, a pantheon of Native American Gods and Deities that represented every one of the North American First Nations. Some were well known, others transcended the realm of tales and oral traditions, but they were all real, watching over the planet and her children, both human and animal.

Grandmother's spirit separated from her body then rose with the blue-violet smoke. She looked down at her own body; the feeling was always disorienting; despite the many times she had performed astral projection. The bewilderment and confusion passed quickly as the sage felt the sensation for rising from her body, skyward.

Grandmother's consciousness soared past the clouds into the night, rising higher into the star-filled sky. The blue-green planet she had loved and protected through the ages shrank to the size of a marble as she flew among the stars.

Traveling beyond the planet's grasp and quickly approaching the silvery white and bluish moon, her journey took her further than any human could imagine. She sped into the cosmos at the speed of thought, rising and away from the Milky Way, until she found herself at what has been christened the 'Pillars of Creation.'

The cosmic marvel was more than towering columns of gas and dust that stretched several light-years tall and housed active stellar configurations. The amber, bronze, and gold formation looked like a weathered butte from the American southwest. As Grandmother 'flew' upwards toward it, her path spun, changing its arc. The Pillars took on another appearance—they looked like a hand. Grandmother smiled as she soared right toward the center, heading straight for the 'palm.' Grandmother knew the profound truth: the Pillars of Creation were not just cosmic formations of gas and dust, but were the fingers and hand of a colossal cosmic entity. This being was so far beyond human comprehension that comparing humans to it was like comparing a grain of sand to the tallest mountain in the vastness of the universe.

Once her consciousness arrived, Grandmother found herself surrounded by an ethereal veil that obscured her view, but through the foggy landscape, she saw the gathering of the Sacred Circle. Each entity was at least four to five hundred feet in height, equaling the Space Needle or the Chrysler Building. Even obscured Grandmother could tell most resembled a hybrid of man & animals.

Grandmother knew that from this perspective, she seemed as minuscule as a grain of sand against the vastness of an ocean. Yet, the Sacred Circle regarded her with respect, recognizing her as their human representative. The towering deities looked down upon her, and she heard their thoughts in her mind.

"We know what has transpired," a booming male voice declared, his eyes glowing with yellow-golden energy.

"Time grows short," a feminine voice intoned, her four slanted, animal-shaped eyes taking on a light green glow.

Grandmother saw the glowing eyes of the Sacred Circle members as they projected their thoughts.

"Yes," Grandmother responded. "Nicholas will be speaking with Alexander soon."

"*He must be made aware of the dangers and the rewards,*" a third thunderous male voice added, emanating a dark blue radiance.

Looking up at the various titans, and without worry in her heart, Grandmother spoke, "I have faith Alexander is worthy. He will prove himself," she declared with conviction. As her words resonated, Grandmother caught sight of one of the colossuses looking down but remaining silent. This divine being, unlike most of his brethren, stayed apart from the others but was present. As Grandmother's words escaped her lips, the immortal's six eyes on three animalistic heads glowed blood-red. Then, it raised its right arm, clenching its fist into a ball of explosive fury. Grandmother knew this would an issue to be resolved another time.

Finally, another female voice among the clouds spoke, "*I hope your aspirations are true, Grandmother, or all is lost.*"

Looking skyward, Grandmother replied, "For generations, humanity has worshipped and believed in you all, no matter what Nation they hailed from. If there was ever a time for the Sacred Circle to have faith in men, specifically one man, it is now." Grandmother stretched out her arms and began moving in a circular pattern at the center of the deities watching her. "I ask you to have faith in Alexander as I do. Though I have not met him yet, I know in my heart and with all that I hold sacred he is the Rainbow Warrior."

TEN

Six hours later, Regino Segel was attempting to relax in his walk-in steam shower. The frameless glass enclosure had oversized, heated dark gray tiles gave the shower a cavern-like feel. Naked, he sat on one of the heated benches, with his back against the outer wall, and spread out. With eyes shut, he remained still to let the steam work into his pores, absorbing the damp heat to sweat out his frustrations.

At the same time Segel's mental gears were spinning—plotting, planning, and preparing. His highest priority was making a deal with the Seneca Nation. To Segel, the other items on his agenda were either lesser matters that could wait or minor irritations.

Segel attempted to clear his mind, seeking a retreat from the pressures of the world and a measure of peace. However, unpleasant memories of his parents, Richard and Julia Segel, always surfaced. These memories were tied to his rise to power, culminating in the moment he killed them.

As Segel sat there, with his mind leaping back and forth between past and the present, while attempting to plan for the future, Macaria crept into the master suite. She peered around the corner to the bathroom, then into the shower, and watched him.

Macaria let the white terry cloth robe drop to the floor, as she wandered into the shower, showing off her tanned and toned naked body. This wasn't the first time the pair had seen each other like this, and they'd grown accustomed to being forward with one another, so Segel wasn't shocked when he opened his eyes and watched her step in, with her cat-like grace, sat down across from him on the opposite bench, then he closed his eyes.

"So, what are you planning?" she asked enjoying the heat, stretching her arms outward, behind her, exposing herself further.

"I need to make an appointment with the Cattaraugus leaders in the next day or so, but I'll also need to speak with the Mayor and let him know S.I. is committed to providing any assistance the city will need at this time."

"That's awfully generous of you. Think your uncle will approve?"

"I think he'll be fine with offering our services. The offer will extend goodwill, especially since S.I. has moved into the region."

"Then what?" Macaria asked, while interlocking her fingers, and stretching her arms above her head, until her joints released a satisfying POP.

After letting out a long sigh, then a deep breath, Segel finally opened his eyes, looking over Macaria's body, with a certain amount of male desire. Reclosing his eyes, and shrewdly smiling, he just said, "Plan B."

ELEVEN

DAY 2

Just after seven, Alex was abruptly awakened from a profound slumber. He felt disconcerted, as though he had emerged from a dense fog. His body was lethargic, his mind disoriented and perturbed, with a persistent darkness lurking at the fringes of his awareness. A surge of adrenaline caused Alex's heart to flutter, but gradually, tranquility enveloped him as he lay swathed in his blankets and comforters, immobilized by choice or circumstance.

Alex moved at a more relaxed pace since he learned he was off for the next few days. While driving Marie home, Alex received a text message from his manager, saying that his call center office was closed.

> Due to the recent weather phenomenon affecting the area, surrounding the company's grounds, due to the proximity to Lake Erie until further notice the Gateway Building will remain closed. The Army Corps of Engineers will be inspecting the grounds within the next week and the building will be examined thoroughly to ensure the safety of all personnel. Once we receive the all clear from officials, we will inform the staff of when we can return to work. Monitor your emails, keep an eye on the news, and stay safe. Alan Garrick

Smart, Alex thought when he read the message. The Gateway Building, about ten years older than Alex, stood roughly a hundred yards from Lake Erie's shoreline. Given the seiche's magnitude, it could have inflicted considerable damage on the seven-story, Art Deco-style building and its foundation, just as it could on every property lining the lake's expanse.

After enjoying a leisurely hot shower and a fast shave, Alex got dressed, opting for his jeans, black boots, and a red and blue, plaid flannel shirt. While eating breakfast, he tuned into the morning news on the TV to check for any overnight developments.

"Good morning, thank you for tuning into Channel 2, Daybreak., I'm Riley Jackson with team coverage after yesterday's unprecedented event of a seiche. Also known as a wave in Lake Erie, which reached an unprecedented size, making its way across the lake into the heart of downtown Buffalo. We have live team coverage from Canalside, the Emergency Management Center, City Hall, and right here, with our own weather team two senior meteorologist, Patrick Hammer, but let's start with the timeline of what occurred."

Alex watched the footage from various cameras along Lake Erie, captured by security cameras from businesses and private lakefront properties on both sides of the river. Each video showed essentially the same thing: the wave moving north towards Grand Island and Niagara Falls, NY, but from different locations along the lake.

Jackson continued.

"At about five p.m. the seiche arrived in Downtown Buffalo, striking the Canalside district, then the remains moved on to the Niagara River, and eventually falling apart somewhere up past Grand Island.

"Relief efforts arrived swiftly, with Buffalo's first responders and volunteers arriving almost immediately. They were quickly followed by meta-human assistance from Queen City's team of Irish heroes, the Garda. Shortly afterwards, Canada's premier team, the Northern Light, arrived to join in the rescue and recovery efforts.

"By six o'clock members of the government sponsored team, the Security Council and Buffalo's group of teenaged heroes, the New Era all appeared to help, by either working on rescue and recovery, or securing areas affected all along the lakeshore, from the Pennsylvania border up to Niagara-on-the-Lake at Lake Ontario."

Alex watched footage of Samhain cast an eerie green light along the waterfront wreckage, searching for survivors. Chinook, a native medicine man and member of Canada's Northern Light, hovered mid-air, casting a spell. Fortune and the Engineer, leader of the New Era, worked together.

The Engineer used his mental control over technology and his mech suit's modular components to create scanners and mechanical limbs, clearing debris for Fortune to rescue survivors. Finally, Charger, the human lightning bolt of the New Era, streaked across the sky.

———

After watching the news, Alex joined his parents on their side of the house, where he found them reading the morning papers, as usual.

"Morning," he said as he walked past the dining room and sat across from them on a beige ottoman near the front window in their sunken living room.

"Good morning," Celeste said, looking up from the USA TODAY, then it crumpled into her lap as she asked, "how'd you sleep?"

Alex noticed the lead story was about the wave and guessed the Queen City would be in the national spotlight for a while. "All right," he answered back. "Aren't you working at the library today?"

"No, I switched with Yvonne, as she has a doctor's appointment tomorrow. So how did everything go last night?"

"Okay, I guess," Alex said unhappily.

Picking up on Alex's melancholy tone, she put the paper aside. "What's that mean?"

"Marie seemed okay, but I'm not sure how she's really doing. I think she's shell-shocked. She took a blow to the head when some idiots freaked out, then pushed her and a few others while bolting for the door," Alex said, then he told his parents everything that happened after Marie called him.

After listening, his mom said, "Maybe you should call her later, just to see how she's doing."

"I considered it, I don't wanna seem pushy or anything, but..."

"But you'd be showing concern," Celeste interrupted him, which was a bad habit of hers.

"I could also check to see if she needs a ride anywhere, because she may have errands to run."

"Don't you have work today?" Reggie asked, lowering the section of the Buffalo News he'd been reading, indicating the conversation finally grabbed his full attention.

"When I was picking Marie up, I got a text from my manager," Alex replied. "The Gateway's closed till it can be checked out by the Army Corp of Engineers, but no telling when that's happening."

Reggie nodded slightly. "Makes sense considering how close the building is to the lake."

"Right, and with the kindergarten and the treatment plant right there, they gotta be sure everything's okay."

"Any idea when they'll be looking at the building?" Mom asked.

Alex shook his head. "Nope. Once they hear something, they'll let us know. Till then all the employees are furloughed."

———

As Alex finished telling his parents what happened the night before, the doorbell rang, and Reggie began pulling himself up out of his recliner, despite Alex offering to answer the door. In a defiant tone, the eighty-five-year-old declared, "I can do it myself," while grabbing his cane, then limped off to the vestibule.

Alex and his mom angrily watched him hobble off, now

needing to support himself after fracturing bones in his right leg, from slipping on ice. The problem was his father believed he was fine and didn't need physical therapy. "Stubborn jackass," Alex muttered under his breath.

Celeste eyed her son, not appreciating his choice of words, but silently agreed with the sentiments. "He'll never change."

"Yup, and it's his fault I'm the same way, between his stubborn streak and your Irish temper, it's a miracle I don't get in more trouble," Alex joked.

Celeste stuck her tongue out at Alex but before he could give her his rebuttal Reggie came back into the living room, pale as a sheet. He could only stammer out, "Alex, it's for you."

Alex rose from the ottoman, as his mother got up from her recliner and immediately went to Reggie's side and whispered, worry in her voice, "What's wrong?"

Reggie didn't answer. All the gray-haired man did was clutch the ivory handle of his ebony cane with a strangling grip.

For Alex, the experience was disconcerting due to the striking resemblance he bore to the elderly Native American standing in the entrance. Despite the old man's silvery ponytail, copper skin tone, and furrowed face, it was clear they were two peas from the same pod. Musing, Alex thought this man—he was related to him biologically, he just knew it. Alex felt as if he was gazing into a funhouse mirror and barely managed to get out two words, "Who are...?" Then, out of the corner of his eye, Alex recognized the second man as the SUV driver.

Alex was about to say something when the man held up a hand, flashing the peace symbol. "Easy, mate. I'm a friend of the family," he offered with a gruff, English accent, then smiled to reassure Alex. "Matter of fact, you could say I'm also hired help."

Turning to face the Harlow family, the older man said, "Alexander, Mr. and Mrs. Harlow, my name's Nick Wolfhart, and this is my friend Orson Dorset." He paused, the weight of the moment evident. Wolfhart then turned back to Alex. "I've imagined this moment for an exceptionally long time, trying to figure out what I'd say, how our first conversation would go. Now that we're face to face, I don't know how to start."

Unsure of where this was headed Alex said the first thing that came to mind. "All right, how about what are you doing here and why was *he* following me?" He glanced at Dorset, who stayed quiet, but smiled.

"What do you mean followed?" Reggie asked.

"I'll explain later, Dad."

"You're right of course, as an old friend of mine says "It's time to piss or get off the pot." Wolfhart stood there looking at his grandson, and so many emotions ran unchecked, like a herd of wild mustangs, but the man forced himself to focus. "Alex, the only way I can tell you this is straightforward, I'm your grandfather, and we need to have a long talk, it's something we can't put off any longer. I know this is a huge shock for you and your parents," Wolfhart continued gesturing towards the Harlows. "But please allow me to explain everything, as you need to hear the whole story. Can we talk? It's necessary and it's crucial."

Alex listened as he stared into Wolfhart's mournful, gray eyes, marked by creases. They were worn out and tired, as if they'd seen too much for one lifetime. Not knowing what else to do, Alex looked at the two people he trusted more than anyone else, and without realizing it his fists balled up on their own, tight and hard, almost forming solid granite. It was an unconscious habit he had when his emotions got the best of him. For a moment the only sound in the living room was his knuckles cracking. The subject of adoption was a delicate one. Unless Alex brought it up, it wasn't mentioned in conversation around him. Bringing it up felt like opening the chute gate on a pissed-off bull at the rodeo.

With the state of shock gone, Celeste said, "Alex, maybe you should listen to them."

Alex let out a long sigh, taking a moment to consider his mother's advice, but he already knew what he'd do. "All right, sit down and start talking." His anger was palpable, visible to everyone. It took every ounce of Alex's self-control to rein in his rage.

"Thank you for listening to me," Wolfhart said, extending a hardened, calloused right hand, which Alex just glared at, then headed back into the living room.

TWELVE

Segel's black, luxury SUV silently pulled up in front of his office in Getzville, a northern suburb around the same time Wolfhart knocked on the Harlow's front door. Segel was silently reading the news & financial sections on his tablet, as Macaria pulled up alongside the sand lime brick building, and directly under the entry canopy on the curved blacktop driveway.

Segel International's Getzville office, located in the Crosspoint complex was the newest addition to the industrial park, neighboring other companies, serving as the northeastern regional headquarters and call center. Meanwhile the search for a facility with manufacturing, warehouse facilities, and access to railways and shipping, that was closer to the city continued.

When the SUV stopped Segel got out, looked at Macaria and said, "Once you park, come upstairs right away. I'm going to need you later."

Looking back at him, with her traditional sly-seductive stare, she answered back, "I just bet you do," then let out a low, growling purr, and smiled slyly.

"This is work, so get your head on straight," he ordered, with a bite in his tone. This was his way of telling Macaria he wouldn't tolerate any distractions, and she got the message when their eyes locked. The industrialist then marched inside, walking past the U-shaped, white marble reception counter, responding with the customary, "Good morning" to the front desk attendant/security staff who greeted him, before proceeding through the security turnstile glass doors to the inner offices. and went straight to the elevators, then to his private office.

A few minutes later Macaria followed, taking off her sunglasses, leaving them inside her black hooded, topper jacket, which she hung inside the coat closet next to Segel's charcoal cashmere topcoat, then slid herself onto the couch. She was dressed in her usual dark outfit; dark gray turtleneck, matching slacks, low heel black boots, and of course she was appropriately armed. The professional stayed silent because Segel was already on the phone with Buffalo's mayor.

"Yes, Mr. Mayor, I appreciate you taking the time to speak with me. I understand how busy you are, so I'll be brief."

"It's true I don't have much time, Mr. Segel. I'm on my way to meet with the city engineers. They've already spoken with the Army Corps of Engineers, but my assistant told me you said this was vital, and with your company bringing business and needed jobs to the region, I agreed to speak with you."

"Believe me, I understand. I have a meeting to get to myself," Segel said as he looked through the smokey, tinted glass, at the regional offices for Fidelis Care and the Cross Point Campus Chapel, in reality he was staring at nothing. Segel began walking around his private office, being on a hands-free device that allowed him to stroll around like a pacing tiger in the cage.

"I wanted to personally let you know Segel International is standing beside the city. You know our resources, the various industries my company covers. If there's anything either the city or any of affected businesses along the waterfront, need for support, do not hesitate to contact me personally. I left my private numbers with your assistant and will be speaking with the leaders of all the communities along the lake's shoreline that may have been affected in some fashion."

Surprised by the generous offer, the mayor responded graciously, "Thank you, Mr. Segel. Right now, we have no idea of the extent of the damage. From my understanding, the determinations will take at least another four or five days for a full examination."

"Once you and your people know what type of assist we can provide, contact me or my personal assistant immediately. We can work out details later. I'm positive we both have a busy day ahead of us, but the vital thing is getting everything back to normal." Macaria instinctively looked at Segel, almost as if she was one of Pavlov's dogs responding to his bell. "And don't worry about cost, as Segel International will donate any materials and resources needed. You have my word."

"Mr. Segel, that's incredibly generous, and I cannot thank you enough for what you are pledging to the city and the people."

"My pleasure Mr. Mayor. I just want you and the other community leaders to know how committed S.I. is to the Western New York area and our being here."

The two leaders exchanged a few more pleasantries and agreed to speak in a few days after the mayor's people knew more. Segel then took the hands-free device from his right ear lobe, and after letting out a long sigh, he ran his hand right over his mouth, then let out a sly smile. *Like playing a fiddle*, he thought. Segal was just really going through the motions with the mayor, but he knew about playing the game and putting on a good public face.

After checking his Rolex, Segel saw he had two minutes before meeting with his Buffalo management team, so he was in no rush. He walked from the windows over to the black wood and chrome valet stand, where he reached down to the accessories shelf, brought up a small bottle of cologne, and gave himself a bit of a spray, then looked in the adjustable mirror, confirming he looked fine.

"So," was the only thing Macaria said, as she looked smugly with her arms instinctively crossed.

Without taking his eyes off his reflection Segel said, "The Mayor's on board, and there's no telling how bad things really are, but he's willing to deal, which means the leaders in the suburbs will deal too." Then he turned to face his valet. "It's one business lesson my uncle taught me, if the largest competitor falls, the others will too."

Macaria nodded slightly, "Makes sense."

"So, are they ready?"

"Yup, your court is in attendance your majesty," she mocked.

He spun on his heels and faced her, "Good, let's go."

————

In a rectangular meeting room, on the second floor, Segel and Macaria strode through the glass door. In front of them were twelve businessmen and women, sitting on both sides of the table. On either end of the table were a pair of office phones and two pop-up electrical outlets, with USB ports. On a side table in the corner, there were three pitchers, two with coffee, one with orange juice, a couple boxes of pastries and doughnuts, with paper plates, napkins, and cups.

"Good morning," Segel strode into the room and claimed his seat at the head of the conference table, a position that commanded immediate attention and respect, with Macaria tiptoeing against the wall behind her employer.

Segel offered a reassuring smile to the five women and seven men, recognizing that the past eighteen hours had likely left everyone on edge. "We have a lot on the agenda to cover but first let me say this; I know right now we're all still anxious after yesterday, but I have news I want to share with you. First, you can spread the word to your various department heads, I just spoke with Mayor Nichols, and I'll be reaching out to other local leaders, whose towns were affected by the wave. I'm committing S.I. to helping the affected communities in any way we can offer. Now at this point we have no idea what this means or what it'll take, at least until we hear back from the communities who need our help.

"Secondly, I'm going to speak with the leaders of the Cattaraugus Reservation for a potential deal with them. I can't disclose the details at this time, but once able, I'll be making a companywide announcement."

A pudgy, balding, white man in a cheap, brown suit sheepishly asked, "Ah, Mr. Segel, I think I can speak for everyone regarding this deal with the Senecas. We're all looking forward to hearing more," he said, as a few others began nodding in agreement. "But when it comes time for our assistance," he continued, "will we be billing the municipalities individually or through Erie County? I think we'd all like to know how this will be handled."

The atmosphere in the room shifted instantly. Tension skyrocketed from two to a fifteen on a ten-point scale as Segel turned and locked eyes with the executive, making everyone uncomfortable. Most of the associates looked anxious, shifting in their seats. A few whispered to their neighbors, pretending to take notes, or checked emails on their phones.

Giving the man a look of disgust, Segel said, "What is your name and what department are you from?" Everyone else stopped cold except for Macaria, who stood silent, snickering enjoying the show.

"Uh, Brooks, Jim Brooks. I'm one of the department heads in manufacturing."

"I see, first I must apologize for not knowing all your names, but I plan to learn them all in time. Being new to the area I haven't had a chance to familiarize myself with personal information." Segel paused for a moment to take a sip of coffee, that had been poured for him. "Mr. Brooks, I'll explain as concisely as I can for you and anyone else who doesn't comprehend what is happening; Segel International will be donating time and materials to those areas affected."

He paused, then slammed his palms down on the table loud enough for everyone to hear. Despite the stinging pain, Segel didn't show any signs he was bothered in the least. "Everything will be donated; time, materials, resources. We will not profit from the misery of our neighbors. I realize this will not be beneficial to our stockholders and some in the company may have issues with my decision, but I don't care. The people in these communities have been touched by an unprecedented disaster. They need help and we will provide whatever help we can.

"I'm new to the area, and I've heard that Buffalo is the city of good neighbors. I'm aware of how people in this region come together, perhaps more so than in other communities. Hell, the people of Western New York have supported communities across the country, whether through donations or manpower. Since S.I. is a new 'neighbor', we're helping out however we can."

Segel then raised his voice to ensure he was heard throughout the second floor. "Now, if anyone has a problem with my decision, I'll discuss it with them later."

The message had been sent, anxiety levels were turned up a few notches, but for Brooks it came across like a direct threat and he looked like he needed to change his shorts.

Macaria had been silent the whole time, just watched the show and smiled. She loved moments like these.

"Now," Segel continued as he sat down, "Like I said, we've a busy agenda to review, so I suggest we table this discussion till later, and attend to the business at hand."

——————

About an hour into the meeting Segel's cell began to vibrate angerly, which he immediately pulled out of his shirt pocket, from under his dark blue/gray vest. His face tightened up and his dark eyes squinted with a renewed focus when he saw the name, Rollins. Immediately Segel stood up, interrupting one of the female executives and announced, "Excuse me everyone, I apologize, but this is a call I have to take," then he headed into the main hallway and back to a secondary, smaller conference room not in use, with Macaria following behind, like a loyal lap dog.

Only after he opened the floor-to-ceiling glass door Segel felt secure enough to swipe up on his phone's screen to accept the call, and only after the door shut behind him, with Macaria standing guard, he felt safe enough to speak. "Go ahead, Rollins."

After a pause Segel said, "I see." His body language made his annoyance clear. Pacing around and balling his right fist, his anger was rising. "That isn't the deal we made.

Tell them if they want the bioagent, they need to pay the agreed price. It's non-negotiable. If they want a discount tell them our deal is off and good luck shopping around for something that's undetectable and can kill three-quarters of a million of their fellow Canadians," then he hung up.

Macaria poked her head inside, and simply asked, "Sounds like Rollins may have a bit more work to do?" Another small smile escaped her blue lipstick covered mouth.

Without looking at his aide, Segel was already planning moves and countermoves, as if he were a grandmaster preparing to face Bobbie Fisher. He seemed to be staring into space when he said, "That is a distinct possibility."

Segel scrolled through his phone, looking up several names and numbers, then texted them to Macaria. "Call these people. They are the President, the Clerk, and the Treasurer of the Senecas, essentially the elected heads of the reservation. There are others involved in the politics, but my preliminary talks have been with these three. Reach out and see if we can schedule our meeting for tomorrow. I need to get back to the staff meeting. I don't know how long it'll take."

Macaria looked at the text and said, "I'll call them now." As she headed back to Segel's office, Macaria asked "I know you have a Plan B in mind in case things don't work out, and Jacob's involved. I'm just dying to know what it is?" She felt confident speaking freely since they were alone.

Segel stood in silence for a moment. His stare was intense and penetrating and, without replying, he returned to the conference room.

THIRTEEN

Everyone was seated in the living room. The Harlows were in their recliners, facing the front wall, where the flat screen was mounted above the gas fireplace. Wolfhart and Dorset sat on the tan, three-person couch that was flush against the wall opposite the bay window. Alex was perched on the window seat to the left of his mother's chair. In the middle of the room, a rectangular brass and glass coffee table, with the ottoman beside it, separating the two sides of the room

"Alex, believe me I understand this is a major shock for you all, and I appreciate what an understatement that is, so please be patient, and I'll tell you everything," Wolfhart said.

Alex sat there in silence, a level of intensity coursing through him like never before. He felt his heart rate accelerate, pumping faster, as though he had just run a marathon. Yet, he remained quiet. Even in stillness, Alex's body language spoke volumes, and it wasn't a conversation for mixed company.

Wolfhart took the accordion folder Dorset was carrying

and handed it to Alex. "These documents will prove I'm telling the truth. Normally, I'd have had to contact an agency—perhaps several—and investigators would have reached out to you. But we have very little time, so Orsen sped things up, and we sidestepped the system. But let me first tell you about your mother. Her name is Ojistah."

"That's beautiful," Celeste said. "I never heard that before. Does it have a particular meaning?"

"Yes, Mrs. Harlow," Wolfhart answered. "It's a Mohawk name, meaning star, and that she is." He turned back to face Alex. "Your grandmother was a full-blooded member of the Mohawk. She wanted to pass down the name to your mother. It's a tradition that's been carried on in their family for generations, but I can tell you more about all that later."

After taking a moment to gather his thoughts the man continued. "When Ojistah told me she was pregnant I didn't take the news well and drove her away. I wasn't ready for her news or to become a grandfather. Our conversation got ugly, and she left the reservation and moved to Buffalo."

Alex's face took on a scowl and his fists balled up again. "Why? I mean why push her away?"

Wolfhart let out a sigh. "Almost a year to the day I lost my wife, and my head wasn't in a good place. My head wasn't in a good place and Ojistah wasn't the only one I pushed away. There's a lot I need to make amends for, believe me."

"Where is she now?" Celeste asked.

Swallowing hard he spoke the bitter truth. "I don't know." An ominous silence entered the room. "After I told her to leave, that was the last I saw of her."

Alex shot daggers directly at Wolfhart from his eyes. "You bastard," was all he could say quietly.

"Alex," she scolded.

"It's alright, I think I understand how he feels," Wolfhart said.

"Don't bet on it, you've no idea how I'm feeling," Alex said, then he shot upright, pointed at Wolfhart, and let loose with both barrels. "I don't know if you're telling me the truth, if we're really related, or if this some kind of a con, bullshitting me. It's not like I'm flush or famous, so I can't figure out what you want. So right now, I can't think of one reason why I shouldn't throw you out of here!" Almost fifty years of pent-up anger at his biological family came to a head, because Alex finally had a target in his sights.

"Alex," Reggie said, his voice booming as he slammed his cane onto the floor, capturing everyone's attention. "This is our house. These men clearly have something to say, and unless they act disrespectfully, you will treat them with courtesy," he declared. Then, turning to his son, finger pointed sternly, he added, "You were raised better than this." The tension in the room reached levels never seen before and Alex just stayed quiet, respecting his father's rules. "Go ahead Mr. Wolfhart," was all Reggie said after Alex's eruption.

"It's all right Mr. Harlow," Wolfhart said extending his hand, in an attempt to keep the peace. "I didn't come here expecting a Hallmark moment." His expression was one of distress and depression, yet he continued. "I knew there might be some hurt feelings, and I don't expect you or your parents to take everything at face value. Examine the records Orsen collected when he was tracking you down. Orson's a trained investigator, and good at his job, and I needed his help, because the state wouldn't release any information about your parents to me."

Alex stayed quiet as he noticed Wolfhart lowered his head but continued. "By the time I was ready to make you part of my life, it was too late, your mother already put you into the system, then vanished."

The tension that once filled the living room had given way to an air of melancholy. After a brief pause, Alex opened the folder and looked over the documents. While he grasped some of them, most were beyond his comprehension, and he realized he would need Marie's help translating everything. What bothered Alex most was the timing; if there was one thing Alex didn't believe in, it was coincidence. Marie's news and Wolfhart showing up in less than twenty-four hours? Alex couldn't buy it.

After giving the documents one last review, Alex bundled them up and handed them to his father, who despite being a retired financial advisor, still had an incredibly sharp mind for the world of business and legal documents that Alex would never be able to comprehend. He was aware that his parents would be interested in the documents, and in time, he also planned for Marie to review them. Knowing his father might not grasp all the details, he looked forward to Marie's assessment. If she approved, Alex would be ready to accept the whole story.

"I'm not saying I believe you, but I need someone I trust to look over these documents. She's an expert in adoption issues. If that's a problem for you, Mr. Wolfhart, then that's regrettable."

Wolfhart responded with understanding, "Trust needs to be earned. Feel free to keep these copies; they are genuine." His tone then became supportive and protective, "I know this is a lot for you and your family. Trust me, I understand more than you may realize." He gave Orson a brief look and added, "As a client of the Homeward Angels agency, it's natural to be curious about your biological family. It will take time, I ask for that time too, to demonstrate my sincerity. I'd like the opportunity to get to know you, as I hope you will want to get to know me."

"I'm not saying I believe you wholly, but you said something about time being a factor. What did you mean?" Alex asked.

"Under normal circumstances, I would have delayed this conversation, especially since Orson is also searching for your mother," Wolfhart explained. "I know this has been a lot for you to take in, but whatever issues we may have, they pale in comparison to what I have to tell you now."

Alex looked at his parents—and the family who looked to be in disbelief, and thought, *How much more is there?*

Reggie questioned, "What are you talking about, Mr. Wolfhart? Is there a medical concern involving Alex, yourself, or his mother?"

"No, nothing like that. I'll try to explain the best way I can." Wolfhart paused again, organizing his thoughts. He knew what he wanted to tell the Harlows but wasn't quite sure how to explain everything to them, let alone make them believe. "Yesterday, that wave was part of what forced me to see you sooner than planned."

"What do you mean?" Alex asked, now more confused than ever.

"I'll give you the condensed version till I can fully explain later, essentially; what happened yesterday was part of a series of natural disasters that are part of a healing process the planet has been going through for some time now, since the mid-nineties. They'll increase in frequency and become more dangerous. This started back in '94, and now time is running short. Several Native peoples and a great many others believe these disasters are part of a healing process, Grandmother Earth is going through, but they're also an indication of what's coming. That man will finally live in harmony with the planet, with the Native Americans leading the way.

"Legends foretell of a destined warrior, a blend of Red man and White man, who will eventually rescue humanity and the Earth. This warrior is said to represent the planet and all human nations. It's believed, Alex, you are this warrior."

Alex appeared to grasp the situation as if it were a joke and seemed ready to respond to Wolfhart.

Wolfhart rose up quickly and placed his arms out in front of him, almost in a begging motion. "Please Mr. Harlow, Alex, I know how this sounds, it's insane even to me, and I've lived my whole life with these stories and the realities. Give me five minutes and I can prove to you I'm telling the truth."

Alex saw his father start to pull himself up out of his recliner and knew he had reached his limit. He also saw something in Wolfhart's eyes that Alex recognized. The man was a believer; he had faith in what he was saying, and nothing Alex could say would dissuade him. Alex wasn't sure if Wolfhart was delusional, lying, or speaking the truth. He stood up and reached out to his father. "Dad, it may seem crazy, but I think we should listen," he said, trusting his usually accurate instincts. "You've got five minutes. Show us your proof," Alex demanded.

"Thank you," Wolfhart replied, undoing the top button of his green and black plaid shirt to reveal the Arrowhead pendant around his neck. "We live in a rather strange world, filled with superhumans akin to modern gods. While I can't account for their origins, for us," he motioned towards Alex, "I know exactly what happened and why we are the way we are. After the first Europeans set foot on this continent, our ancestors were entrusted with a hallowed responsibility to safeguard the survival of both the planet and humanity.

"My great, great, great, great, great grandfather was the first Warrior to be given this pendant." Wolfhart handed the arrowhead to Alex, who took a good long look at it as his grandfather continued. "Every member of our bloodline has the power inside them, and this is the key to unlock it. Now believe me, I understand how this sounds, and how you might be feeling. When my father told me the same story, I felt the same way, that he was out of his mind, but once I show you the path, Alex, you'll be capable of things you can't imagine.

"What exactly do you mean? What are you talking about?"

"When we unlock this power, we bridge a gap between humanity and our animal brethren. We gain the strength of the grizzly, the speed of a cougar, the senses of a wolf, the eagle's vision, and Alex," Wolfhart began, his smile broadening, "For you, this is only the beginning."

Alex, who had been absorbed on the pendant's center, where a wolf howled, lost himself in the moment. Handing back the pendant, he inquired, "What is this about?"

"Legend says only the warrior can harness the remaining powers at his disposal. It's all about aiding you in mastering the abilities of your mind and soul," Wolfhart explained.

Reggie, ever the skeptic, was running out of patience. "Time's up. Where's this proof you mentioned? Show us now."

"Mr. Harlow, let me show you exactly what I'm talking about, and hopefully you'll believe as well." Wolfhart held up the pendant in his hand, put it to his chest, and concentrated. His breathing grew faster, his blood flowed quicker, and suddenly his body changed. It took on the same shimmering, aura, it did when he demonstrated for Orson. Wolfhart's physical vitality was restored, making him stronger and faster than Alex and Dorset combined. But the clincher for the Harlows saw how Wolfhart's eyes changed, taking on an avian appearance.

Orson, knowing what was happening, allowed himself a small smile, because he knew in a moment the Harlow family would believe.

———

When Alex first put the arrowhead around his neck, he felt ridiculous, and could barely believe Wolfhart's stories, first about being his grandfather, let alone that he was supposed to be a world savior. But there was no denying what he and his parents just saw.

"Is he going to be alright?" Celeste asked, visibly concerned about her son's safety, then began shaking her head. "I don't think you should do this, Alex."

"Yes, ma'am," Wolfhart answered. "I had the same concerns, not only for myself when my father passed the Arrowhead down to me, but also when Ojistah wore it. Believe me, I wouldn't risk her safety any more than you would risk Alex's."

"She did?" Alex asked, surprised to hear his mother had borne the same responsibilities he was now being asked to assume.

"Yeah, she began her journey as Wildrun, a local hero-ine, around 1961. However, when she discovered she was pregnant with you, she decided to retire her mask and costume, back in 1969. Perhaps your parents have mentioned her?"

Reggie responded, "I recall Wildrun. I saw her once downtown, must have been around, oh, 1967 I think, she was fighting that criminal—what was his name?" he asked, struggling to recall, then it came to him. "Ah, Rustbelt, the half-man, half-machine."

Wolfhart agreed, "Yes, she was excellent, even better than me in some ways."

"What do you mean?" Alex asked.

"Oh, it's nothing."

"Bollocks," Orson interjected. "I've been here, listening to everyone and stayed quiet because it wasn't my place. Aside from your mother, Nick was also a hero in his own time." Alex and the Harlows shifted their attention to Wolfhart, who stayed modestly quiet. Dorsett stood up and carried on, "Back in the late forties and fifties, your grandfather was also dashing about in a costume, akin to your mother, but he was known as the Red Warrior."

"The Red Warrior?" Celeste asked. "You were the Red Warrior?" Dumbfounded was the only word to describe her reaction.

"Yes, I was."

"Reggie, you remember I told you how the Red Warrior saved my father from being attacked by a group of those Hitler supporters during the war."

"Oh yeah, right," Reggie said.

"What?" Alex asked.

"Yes, I must have mentioned that," Celeste went on. "Your grandfather, uh, my father that is, wouldn't assist these brownshirts, the Aryan Assembly, in tapping into the phone lines," she added swiftly, detailing her father's job as a lineman for the telephone company. She recounted how this group of Axis supporters attempted to establish a foothold in the Buffalo area. After her father told the group no, he was ambushed by some of their members. However, the Red Warrior intervened and dealt with them back in 1942, when Celeste was just a year old.

Smiling bashfully, Wolfhart said, "I'm sorry Mrs. Harlow I don't remember the details, but it sounds familiar. I'm just glad I could help your father."

"I remember reading about the Red Warrior and Wildrun in a book on local metahumans a few years ago. It featured a chapter on Native Americans that spanned a considerable period. Another section mentioned how the Red Warrior fought a communist threat in the fifties," Alex remembered. "What was his name? Oh yeah," Alex said as he snapped his fingers, "The Red Menace and his partners."

"Well, that was a long time ago," Wolfhart said. "It's ancient history, and we can discuss it later." His voice took on a serious tone. "Alex, it's time."

Locking eyes with the man, Alex conveyed his final acceptance with a subtle nod. He closed his eyes and followed Wolfhart's instructions, murmuring, "Nothing to it, but to do it."

Wolfhart explained Alex needed to reach out to his spirit guides and as he did this, he took a small package from his pocket, opened it up and poured green and brown powder in his hand.

Initially, Alex's breaths were slow and shallow as he cleared his mind, just as Wolfhart had advised.

Approaching Alex, Wolfhart reassured, "Just breathe deeply. It won't harm you; it's safe and will aid in contacting your guides. They will show you the necessary path." With that, he blew the powder into Alex's face.

Alex inhaled the herb mixture, as the others watched, not sure what to make of what they were seeing. The herb combination smelled like a fusion of pine and moss, with spices and some sweetness Alex couldn't place.

With closed eyes, Alex's breathing quickened, as did his heartbeat. Then, Alex began to discern shapes materializing in his mind. Confusion took hold as his hands clenched, and he spoke out loud, "What is that?"

The shapes merged into trees and a mountain range emerging from a swirling mist. The scene resembled a campground Alex visited as a child but hadn't thought about in a very long time.

Alex smelled the pine trees and felt a gentle breeze. The path's dirt shifted beneath his feet as he walked, and the reality of the situation eluded him; it felt authentic, yet it wasn't.

A veil of misty fog enveloped the area, partially obscuring the view. Alex walked ahead, struggling to believe the unfolding events, yet certain that everything Wolfhart had revealed was indeed true.

Ahead in the distance, a large, indistinct shape loomed through the fog, moving on all fours. Alex felt a surge of fear, but it dissipated as he reassured himself, "You're in the living room. You're still at home." Repeating this mantra, he advanced towards the mysterious figure. As he neared it, the foggy silhouette sharpened into a wolf, larger than any he had seen before. Alex noticed an abnormality; its back was deformed, giving it a hunchbacked appearance. He discerned the ears and face of the gray, white, and black creature, yet its legs and claws were unlike any wolf's. When it stood before him, the truth dawned on him: this was no ordinary wolf. The supposed hunch was a pair of folded wings, and its legs were as robust as those of a grizzly bear. The wolf stood motionless, its gaze piercing directly into Alex's eyes, reaching into his soul. The wings unfurled, resembling those of an eagle, yet with a wingspan surpassing any known bird of prey. As the wings fully spread, Alex was in for a larger shock when two more animal heads emerged as the creature stood upright like a man. On the right was a grizzly bear; on the left, a mountain lion. In its full splendor, this hybrid creature evoked images of the Sphinx and the Griffin in Alex's mind.

The beast unleashed a baying howl that reverberated endlessly. The intensity of the creature's gaze on Alex was unimaginable. Approaching Alex, the creature kept its eyes fixed on him, undergoing an astonishing transformation. Its body morphed from animalistic to humanoid from the neck down, yet it retained its gray and black fur and sharp claws. Once its metamorphosis ceased, it towered over Alex, standing nearly fourteen feet tall—triple Alex's size. Adorned with a feathered necklace, earrings that dangled from its head, and a loincloth of green and brown accented with red and gold trim, it also sported matching wristbands and tan-gold leggings. The transformation made it a hybrid of a werewolf and an eagle.

Gazing down at Alex, it extended an arm behind its back to retrieve a spear, almost twenty-feet in length, the weapon had a head resembling an upward-sticking silvery eagle feathers on either side of the blade, giving it a trident-like appearance, complete with eagle feathers trailing from the shaft. The creature stepped closer to Alex, and part of him admittedly was afraid, but even more so, he was fascinated, and thought to himself, *my God.*

"I am not the deity you worship, nor any god you may know," the creature's voice echoed in Alex's mind. *"The Lakota call me Shunkaha Wakinyan, Wolf-With-Wings-Of-Thunder. I am your guide, and your journey has just commenced."* With that, Shunkaha Wakinyan touched his left claw to Alex's shoulder. *"I know of your mother, I know of your grandfather, and I know your family's history. I was there in the beginning; I will be there at the end. Some have called the calling a blessing, others a curse. All I can tell you is it is your destiny. I will walk the path with you. I will advise you when I can. Know that this journey will not be easy. It will be challenging at times, but it will be rewarding beyond imagination. After the darkness recedes, seek out Grandmother. She will illuminate the remainder of your path and bestow upon you the full breadth of your abilities. Until the morrow."*

Just as Alex was about to ask about Grandmother, Shunkaha Wakinyan moved his claw from Alex's face to his chest and, without warning, struck, slashing Alex's chest. Alex felt the raking sensation penetrate his body and screamed out in shock.

Shunkaha Wakinyan then grasped his spear, hoisted it above Alex's head with both hands, and thrust it downward. Instinctively, Alex raised his arms to shield himself, momentarily forgetting that he was on the spiritual plane, not the mortal one. At that instant, he snapped out of his trance and found himself back in the living room with the others.

———

After finally catching his breath, with beads of sweat breaking out all over his body, and a shocking chill running through his insides, Alex had one question: "Why me?"

Wolfhart looked at his grandson with a woeful expression and could only answer as honestly as possible, "I don't know. I wish I had all the answers, but I don't." A heavy silence fell as the intensity of the moment lingered in the room.

"Grandmother," Alex finally whispered.

"What's that?" Celeste inquired.

"I said Grandmother," he repeated, then described everything that happened. "This thing, whatever it is, said I need to see someone called Grandmother, whoever she is."

Wolfhart explained, "Grandmother's our medicine woman and spiritual leader on the reservation. Who told you to speak with her?"

"Someone, something, calling itself Shunkaha Wakinyan," Alex replied.

"You're positive?" Wolfhart asked, his face a mix of concern and astonishment.

"When you come face to face with something that's four-teen feet tall, a cross of a wolf, a bear, and an eagle, bran-dishing a spear at your head, you're gonna remember it, believe me," Alex retorted. "Now tell me, who or what is Shunkaha Wakinyan?"

"Shunkaha Wakinyan is a deity of the Lakota Sioux, though not widely known. His name translates to "Wolf With-Wings-of-Thunder" and is believed to be one of the first ones, one of the entities that created the cosmos and defended the world ages ago from creatures only known as The Dark Ones. I know how this all sounds, but I've learned all legends have some basis in truth." Then Wolfhart focused right on Alex., "If Shunkaha Wakinyan is your guide and told you, that you need to talk with Grandmother, you need to speak with her as soon as possible." Then he began shaking his head in disbelief at what Alex said. "To be honest, son, I'm amazed because Shunkaha Wakinyan is one of the most powerful of gods. If he is your spirit guide that is beyond amazing, believe me."

"Are you saying there's more than one God?" Celeste asked. As a devout Catholic, this concept was harder for her to grasp than Alex being a metahuman.

"Yes, ma'am," Wolfhart replied. "I understand this may be difficult to believe, but I need you to trust me on this, and much more."

Ever the skeptic, Reggie had heard enough and reached his limit. He pointed his cane directly at Wolfhart's face and declared, "No, we don't. You've come here with some cock-and-bull story, shown us tricks any good magician could pull off, and expect us to hand over our son to you?" He punctuated his refusal by driving the tip of his cane into the floor. "No, sir. Until your claims are verified by the authori-ties, I think it's best you leave."

"Except for one thing, Dad," Alex cut in with. "My run-in with Shunkaha Wakinyan."

"What are you talking about?"

Alex stood up and unbuttoned his shirt. "This," he revealed. He took off his shirt, exposing proof he told the truth. Fresh claw marks trailed down his upper left torso, similar to those inflicted by a grizzly bear. Across Alex's broad chest were five new, crimson gashes, deep and wide, their slightly elevated edges marking the beginning of recovery.

"Oh, my God," Celeste gasped, getting out her chair. "Are you all right?"

"What happened?" Reggie demanded. "When did you get those gashes? We need to call a doctor or get you to the E.R.," he exclaimed, his voice almost reaching an uncharacteristic pitch of panic.

"I'm fine, everyone," Alex replied, assuring his family, sounding amazingly calm for the situation, then turned around for all to see. "It happened just as I described: Shunkaha Wakinyan slashed at me, struck me with his spear, then I found myself back here, in my body. These marks weren't here before I took my little 'trip'. When I regained consciousness, I knew something was different, and I could feel them, but they don't hurt." Alex turned to Wolfhart. "Any ideas?"

Wolfhart studied the scars with a puzzled expression. "I can't explain this. Perhaps Grandmother will have an answer. We should seek her counsel. It's possible you've been singled out by the deities, placed under their vigilant gaze." Changing the subject, Wolfhart inquired, "Alex, think back on what happened. What do you remember?"

"What exactly?" Alex inquired.

"Despite everything, try to remember any sounds, scents,

or sights you experienced, not with Shunkaha Wakinyan, but here, in our realm."

Alex shook his head as he began to put his shirt back on. "Nothing really," he said, pausing to reflect for a moment before continuing. "The last thing I remember, after inhaling those herbs or whatever they were, is feeling like my back was breaking and every muscle straining, almost like being hit with a taser. I couldn't move or think, but..." His voice trailed off as he let his thoughts wander.

"What is it, Alex?" his mother inquired.

"I don't know," he replied, his head turning as if on a swivel, then he faced Reggie. "Dad, I don't have the proof you're looking for, and I can't explain what's happening any more than Wolfhart can, but you've seen these scars, and all I can say is that this is all real."

Despite not understanding the situation, the sight of Alex's face made Reggie finally accept that it was real.

————

After the situation had calmed and arrangements for the next day were made, Alex accompanied Wolfhart and Dorset to their car. During the walk, Wolfhart attempted to lessen the gap between them. Alex agreed to meet with Wolfhart at the Reservation the next day. "I wasn't certain how to convince you had you declined," he confessed.

"Once I make up my mind, I'm a tough nut to crack, and seldom change my mind," Alex replied, his earlier animosity dissipated. "But once I commit, I follow through, no matter what. I may not understand what's happening, but I'll meet this Grandmother and hear her out; hopefully she'll shed light on some of my questions."

"That's all I can ask."

"Seems to me you're asking a lot," Alex observed.

Wolfhart found himself unable to argue with Alex, yet he clung to the hope of nurturing a closer relationship, knowing it would take time—a luxury they both wished for.

"Alex," Wolfhart said, "the only thing I can assure you of is that Grandmother will guide you to have your heart weighed. You'll be tested in unprecedented ways. Pass, and the 'lock' will open forever."

"What if I fail?" Alex inquired.

Wolfhart shook his head gravely. "I'm not going to lie to you, I honestly don't know."

———

After watching Wolfhart and Orsen drive away, Alex stood in the driveway, the arrowhead clenched in his fist, swinging rhythmically. Overwhelmed by what happened and the weight of responsibilities few could comprehend; Alex grappled with his emotions. Once his anger towards Wolfhart subsided, the pent-up feelings surged, prompting him to retreat to the seclusion of the family's backyard where Alex succumbed to the turmoil within and vomited behind the privacy fence.

The gravity of the situation weighed on Alex's mind as he headed back into the house, having caught his breath and wiped the cold sweat from his brow. He joined his parents back in the living room but kept his distance, due to his breath. He intended to brush his teeth and take an antacid to settle his stomach, but knew they would want to discuss everything that happened.

"So, Mr. Wolfhart went back home?" Celeste asked.

Just looking into space Alex said, "Yeah," after a slight pause.

"Any idea what you're going to do?" she asked.

"You saw my scars, so you know what I went through

was real," Alex said as he faced his parents. "There's no denying what I went through." Clutching the arrowhead, he looked at it intently before continuing. "We live in a strange world where plenty of mysterious things happen. I had some time to think, and something has changed in me. I know I'm not the same. The only way to describe it is that I've seen and heard things that are beyond explanation. I kept silent before because I felt somewhat... loopy, for lack of a better word. But when I returned," he gestured with air quotes, "I realized my senses were heightened."

"What do you mean?" his dad asked, clutching his cane's handle even while seated, his right leg stretched out in front of him.

"For a moment, my hearing seemed sharper than usual, and my sense of smell too," he added.

"I'm not sure I understand." Celeste said.

"Did you apply your arthritis cream today? The one with vanilla and gardenia?" Alex asked.

She nodded slightly, "Yes, but how did you know?"

"It has a distinctive scent I recognized," Alex clarified.

Surprise crossed Celeste's face. "There's no way you could've known that; I applied it nearly six hours ago on my knees."

"Best I can figure," Alex reasoned, "Is I detected the lingering scent of the cream."

"Alex," Reggie cut in, "I think we need a lawyer to review these documents. I want to verify everything this man claims. I'm going to call my former business partner, you remember Bob…" Alex nodded. "He'll know who we can contact. I don't want you speaking to this man, at least till we speak to someone, maybe even your caseworker."

"That's a problem, because I need to meet up with this Grandmother, whoever she is."

The elder Harlow started to shake his head, "No, I don't

think that's smart." To underscore his point, he drove his cane down, as he had done previously.

Alex shook his head in turn. "Sorry, this is something I have to do," then gave a wave with his right hand. Anticipating the barrage of objections from Reggie, Alex spoke up before either of his parents could. "The only way to explain it is like this: not only did I give him my word." Alex knew his parents understood the significance he placed on keeping his word. "But, after Shunkaha Wakinyan marked me and ordered me to meet Grandmother, I knew instantly it's where I had to be. It's not a choice, Dad. Believe me, the same alarms are going off for me too, hell more for me than you guys, but this is necessary. I have to be there, even if it means confronting a man I don't trust. That's just how it has to be."

"I don't like this, and I'm calling Bob today to see if he can recommend someone immediately."

"I don't have a problem with that, so call him and see if he knows someone, but I'm going. Like I said, I don't have a choice."

To break the tension his Mom asked, "What time are you going?"

"I figure around ten." After a moment, he continued. "I'm going to call Marie and give her a heads-up about this to see if she has heard or knows anything," he said.

Celeste looked puzzled. "Why?"

"She might know something or recognize Wolfhart's name. At the very least, when we get my files, we'll have a starting point."

"That's true," Celeste agreed.

Alex stood up. "I'd better call her, at the very least I can see how she's doing." Then he went to make his call after he brushed his teeth.

"What are you going to tell her?" she asked.

"Only what I have to, the bare minimum. No way I can explain to her what's happening, especially since I don't understand it myself."

———

After they were alone, Celeste turned to Reggie and asked, "What are you thinking?"

Reggie sat there for a minute or two in silence. "I don't know."

Celeste gazed at her husband, and in Reggie's eyes, she saw worry and fear. "I don't know either, but Alex is level-headed, and as you've often said—he's smarter than you are and has a bigger heart than I do." She concluded, "We have to have faith Alex will be fine."

"Amen to that," Reggie replied softly. "I'm going to call Bob," he declared. He rose and made his way to his office at the back of the house, adjacent to their bedroom. Reggie experienced all the same feelings as Celeste, but kept them under control, now recognizing that the world was vastly bigger and more complex than they had ever realized. They were aware that times had changed since the 1940s of their youth, but they could never have imagined that Alex would become part of such an unfamiliar new world.

———

After rinsing out his mouth and throat, and brushing his teeth, Alex sat down on his love seat, grabbed his cell and called Marie's house phone, which she had given him after they got to her cottage.. All he got was her voice mail, so all he could do was leave a message. "Marie, ah, it's Alex. I hope you're okay. Ah, I was wondering if you could call me later. I gotta ask you something, and no, this doesn't have anything to do with yesterday. You can call me anytime, thanks."

Alex closed his eyes and tried to calm his mind down. Everything that happened in the past fifty hours spun around in his memories and he couldn't shut them down. *Why me? I don't want any of this! Don't I get a say? It's not fair! I was never asked; that bastard just assumed I'd take charge!*

Once Alex had calmed himself, he acknowledged that despite his disdain for the situation, he relished the newfound strength. He hadn't confessed to anyone that he felt stronger than ever before, and he secretly enjoyed it. Alex realized he might come to appreciate certain aspects of this predicament, perhaps even embrace them, which frightened him.

FOURTEEN

Five and a half hours later, Segel returned to his office, sporting an intense look that was uncharacteristic of him. "So," he uttered to Macaria.

She had been awaiting Segel's return with the patience of a loyal guard dog, reclining on the chrome-framed, black leather couch, legs crossed, engrossed in Candy Crush on her cellphone. "I managed to persuade the Three Stooges to meet with you tomorrow. It's set for ten-thirty," she informed him.

Segel closed and locked the door, then said, "Good girl," and proceeded to lower the blinds beside the office door.

Rising with a smirk, Macaria inquired, "So, what's your plan for tomorrow?"

Approaching Macaria, Segel gazed into her sparkling violet eyes and smiled. "If the Seneca leaders won't negotiate, Jacob will step in." He gave Macaria a look that she knew all too well.

Without hesitation she ripped open his dress shirt, scattering the buttons everywhere.

The pair shared many traits; ambitiousness, ruthlessness,

efficiency, creativity, and had a love for wealth and power. Macaria was comfortable with the no-strings-attached relationship with her boss, feeling indebted to him for rescuing her from the trailer parks of Texas and transforming her into a formidable woman. She was committed to the journey, regardless of the direction things took with Segel.

Segel unbuckled Macaria's belt, then pulled down her dark slacks, and ran his fingers up in-between her legs. She said with a quiver in her voice, "Tell me what you're going to do if they won't deal."

As Segel slid his fingers into Macaria's G-string, he revealed Plan B. "If they won't agree to play ball, Jacob will use one of the untraceable, next-generation explosives from our weapon's division. You can surmise the rest."

"Ooooohhh," Macaria moaned out loud. "Nice, then what?"

Segel continued to tease her and felt her warm excitement. "Jacob has worked on files he'll upload to their computers, of working on a new casino deal, that New York State would never approve of. This in turn will make it look like a someone on the state gaming commission wanted this deal to fall apart and killed the leaders to stop them from acting."

"Very nice," Macaria said. She took him by the hand, and began walking backwards, leading Segel back to the couch, as she unzipped his slacks and ran her hand inside feeling how excited he'd become. "Come here," she ordered him.

On top of power and money, the third thing the pair had in common was that violence was a serious turn on for them both. The idea of eliminating the Seneca leaders and making the deal happen was enough to keep the pair busy the rest of the afternoon and into the night, until after the staff left.

FIFTEEN

Throughout the day, Alex remained alone, attempting to make sense of the events that had unfolded. Accepting the reality was challenging, but eventually he reconciled Wolfhart's words. In addition to keeping his word, Alex's adaptability was a key trait; a skill honed over many years. Moreover, he was a survivor. A cousin once joked that in the event of a nuclear holocaust, only cockroaches and Alex would remain. He meant that Alex could withstand anything the world threw at him, good or bad, and still somehow emerge victorious. After today, Alex understood that he would need all these skills to confront the impending challenges.

Throughout the rest of the afternoon and into the early evening, Alex spent time online conducting research in his office, previously an examination room when the wing served as a doctor's office. He delved into the history of the heroine Wildrun. His curiosity about her was understandable, yet this represented a completely new facet of Ojistah that Alex felt an urgent need to explore.

The initial website Alex explored was Metacatalog,

acclaimed as the ultimate online compendium for the most comprehensive assortment of superpowers known to humanity. This Who's Who, with over 200,000 pages of intricate details, scrupulously records and classifies every metahuman disclosed, along with their recognized abilities, affiliations, adversaries, and the notable incidents or occurrences they participated in. After typing in Wildrrun's name in the search bar, Alex learned about his mother's heroic career.

Starting in the early sixties, Wildrun first appeared by thwarting a bank robbery near the Reservation in Irving. Within a year, she battled Buffalo's superpowered fascist, the Kaiser, a remnant of World War II. She also defeated Rustbelt, a cyborg capable of inducing a rust-like effect on metal. Over the following eight years, Wildrun fought criminal groups such as the original Common Council, the Nature Preserve, and Route Five, either by herself or in collaboration with other heroes like the human-animal hybrid The Griffin, the Lackawanna street vigilantes, the Baker Boys, or the region's premier superhero team, The Stampede, which included Republic Steele, Rockpile, the Norseman, Skyway, and Silver Arrow.

Alex found four photos of Wildrun on the website, all depicting her against various villains during public battles or captured by a photographer while rescuing a family from a car wreck near Derby, NY. He'd hoped for some clearer images and attempted to zoom in for a closer look at her face, but the photos became blurry when enlarged.

A fanboy's charcoal rendering of her possible close-up appearance also had been uploaded. When Alex saw it, he was uncertain of his feelings. Despite the mask in the image, he could discern his mother's beauty. To Alex, she appeared striking, proud, and defiant, yet there was warmth in her expression and eyes. Alex knew he needed to talk with

Wolfhart about the rendering's accuracy in comparison to any real photographs the man might possess.

———

After several hours of research on both Wildrun and the Red Warrior, Alex checked the time, and it was already half past seven and dark outside. He lost track of time and the ache and stiffness in his legs let him know it was time to move around.

Alex felt a breeze wafting through the sliding window of his office, signaling mid-fall when days grow cooler and nights turn chilly, yet the weather remained agreeable in Western New York. Restlessness took hold of Alex and he knew a drive was the only remedy to clear his mind. On such drives, his destination was unknown, the duration uncertain. Celeste had once asked him about these solitary journeys, to which Alex had simply replied, "I never know where I'm heading; I let the winds guide me."

Alex slipped on his dark blue zip-up vest, grabbed his wallet and car keys, and headed out. He didn't make it a habit to inform his parents of his comings and goings. It'd almost seem as if he was asking permission, like he was still sixteen, just after getting his driver's license. He knew this wasn't true, yet living again at his parents' home cast a different light on things. Occasionally, he wrestled with the feeling that he would never fully step into the role of the man he believed he was meant to be.

Outside in the driveway, Alex started his Charger, which he believed emitted a low purr or growl, reminiscent of awakening from a cold start or idling at a red light. However, when he revved the engine, it roared with a primal and aggressive tone, akin to a predator about to strike or battling for survival.

The roads were quiet, and Alex found himself alone on the streets, except for the sporadic vehicle in South Buffalo. Many were still reeling, opting to remain near their loved ones. A little over an hour passed before he reached the vicinity of Ripley, NY, and then he decided to turn back, making his way northward to the city.

Normally Alex drove with music, this was one of those times he drove in silence. He needed to clear his mind, time to think in silence.

It was almost nine-thirty when Alex found himself approaching the West Seneca border. Once he realized it, he floored the accelerator, propelling the Charger up an on-ramp and heading straight for downtown, unaware of his destination.

About ten minutes later, Alex found himself in the heart of downtown, near the Pearl Street Brewery approaching Sahlen Field, home of the Buffalo Bisons. As Alex drove through the urban canyons of Downtown Buffalo, he noticed two things: first, the area seemed to be deserted; and secondly, bright orange flashing lights caught his attention. They were D.P.W.'s barricades, blocking traffic from Marine Drive and areas close to the waterfront.

As Alex passed between Harborcenter and the former home of the Buffalo News, he noticed a slight fog rolling in and slowly spreading. He made a left turn and passed in front of the Key Bank Center, finally realizing he was right back where he had picked up Marie, with the emergency camp just a block up on the left. The one-way traffic wasn't in place, but there were still emergency workers and authorities using the parking lot as a temporary work site. To avoid all the activity, Alex made a right onto Illinois Street and headed towards the Cobblestone District, planning to connect with South Park and head back home. But as they say, the best-laid plans of mice and men often go awry.

On Alex's right was the Key Center's parking structure, that almost ran the length of the block. To his left were several brew pubs, taverns, and after-hours establishments that helped revitalize the historic district, and as Alex cruised towards South Park, four individuals ran diagonally, across the street, in front of the Charger, and Alex had to slam his breaks, otherwise he'd have hit them.

Two of them passed right in front of his headlights. Alex immediately recognized them by their gang colors and the red and blue "TX" on the back of their black or gray hoodies, just like the ones he had seen on the news. They were members of the Trax, a street gang that had established their activities near the old Central Terminal on Buffalo's east side. Typically, they avoided heading downtown and to South Buffalo, sticking to the east side and the Riverside neighborhood. Over the past few years, the group's power had increased significantly.

With his driver's window down, Alex heard the gang yelling back and forth. "Move it 8-Ball," the one leading the pack yelled back to the straggler, the largest of the four, who struggled to keep up.

"All right, get off my ass," 8-Ball yelled back, ignoring Alex and trying to keep up with his cronies. Being the biggest and slowest, it wasn't easy. "Chill, man, no rush. Those rides ain't moving, and the cops ain't anywhere near here."

Alex watched them in his rear-view mirror and saw the quartet run straight for the parking structure. He quickly guessed that if the Trax were operating downtown, it wasn't for a trip to the Seneca Casino or the Harbor Center. They were looking to boost cars left behind after the seiche, and something felt off for him. Under normal conditions, Alex would have called the police and gone straight home. Now something had changed. There was no presence of the police or any of the heroes that had been downtown. According to the news, law enforcement was stationed near the Naval & Military Park, along Marine Drive, at the intersections of Main and Hanover Streets, which were several blocks away.

Overwhelmed by an unusual impulse, Alex was acutely aware of, he kept his gaze on the gang members as they ran into the unattended building. Although the group was out of sight, Alex could hear their shrill laughter reverberated off the brick and cement. Alex narrowed his eyes, sharpening his focus to disregard the glaring, pale-orange streetlights.

What the hell are you doing? he asked himself. *This is none of your business. Just go home. Someone will stop them — the cops or one of the heroes running around.* But it quickly became clear that nobody was coming to stop the Trax. The only person around was Alex.

Alex parked at the curb on one of the few remaining streets in the city that still had exposed cobblestones. He got out of his car as his instincts slowly took over, but these weren't his normal impulses, they were unfamiliar, and Alex didn't realize what was happening at first. Without realizing it, Alex reached for the arrowhead still in his jeans' pocket with his right hand. As soon as he did, he felt the charge run through his body, unleashing the power inside him.

Alex's muscles felt like they gained mass, becoming denser, harder. His lungs took in more oxygen than ever before, it seemed as if he was hyperventilating, but in reality, his body was super-oxygenating his blood. Then Alex's senses reached unparalleled levels, and for a moment, it all became too much for him. The waterfront scents of saltwater and dead fish, combined with the aromas from the GM Plant producing Cocoa Puffs, flooded Alex's nostrils. It was an intense experience, and despite his attempts to shut out the world, he found it inescapable.

In those moments, Alex's mind was on the verge of shutting down, overwhelmed as a form of protection, when suddenly, a voice from the recesses of his mind commanded him to act.

Focus! Your body and senses will adjust in time. You must stop those vermin before they prey on the innocent!

It was Shunkaha Wakinyan's voice again, but this time, Alex wasn't consumed by fear, shock, or awe. Instead, he was imbued with determination, purpose, and grit.

Alex looked back towards the parking ramp, almost three hundred yards away, but he saw it clearly, despite having the night and a slight fog on their side.

Alex's first reaction was one of total disbelief and astonishment at how clearly he saw all the way to the end of the block, which was almost two football fields away, at night. Alex didn't think, he just followed his instincts. His right fist clenched up, then ran full out, faster than he ever moved before. At first, Alex moved at a normal pace, but he quickly built-up speed, and for a moment, it seemed as if the world stood still. In less than twenty seconds, he reached the entrance/exit gate the Trax members had run through. Alex amazed himself when he realized he wasn't slowing down and leapt over the white-and-black striped gate arm connected to the lot attendant's booth.

Alex cleared the arm but instinctively ducked his head, thinking he might whack it on the concrete level above him. Once he stuck the three-point landing on his feet and braced himself with his fist, he realized he was still rising higher than he had ever jumped before. As Alex came down, he instinctively crouched, the way a mountain lion would when it lands, and barely felt the impact as his feet hit the wet cement rampway.

His focus shifted because Alex was overwhelmed by his senses, impacting his mind at the same time. His wolf-like sense of smell detected the street punks and Alex thought *Uggghhhhh*, when he picked up on their individual body odors, which were beyond repulsive. Instinctively, Alex's head twitched, and he thought he'd gag from their lack of hygiene.

At the same time, thanks to his eagle-like vision, Alex clearly saw everything despite his vision being slightly disoriented by the ultraviolet spectrum. He waited a moment for his eyes to adjust. The orange streetlights downtown irritated him. He had never been this photosensitive before, but now the brightness really bothered his eyes. Alex winced against the glaring light whenever he could. He also saw almost translucent waves of light blue and violet, like specters. These visions would come and go, almost disappearing into the darkness. Alex figured he would need to talk to Wolfhart or Grandmother about his eyesight.

Finally, Alex's wolf hearing heard the pack leader across the first level, as far as Alex was concerned, he might as well have been using a bullhorn.

"8-Ball, you and Mack hit those cars over 'dere. Jigger and I will get these two," he ordered. "Ya' know what 'da boss is lookin' fer."

Alex caught up with the group, who were in front of a bunch of cars, further down on Level One. They were almost on top of the next entrance booth, and Alex stood there watching the thieves begin to work. His right fist balled up on its own, loud enough to crack his knuckles, and let the Trax know they weren't alone.

"What the hell," 8-Ball yelled out, as the gang members all looked up from the two cars they were breaking into.

Alex stood there, channeling his anger but trying to stay calm. His head was tilted downward so the Trax couldn't get a clear look at his face, then he said, "The city's dealing with the fallout, and you bastards decide to target the victims?" His anger became an animalistic fury that quickly rose, and Alex knew he was about to unleash it. "You've preyed on the innocent for way too long, now you're all going to learn what it means to be the prey."

Without another word, Alex leapt at the closest pair, ten feet away, and no one would forget what happened next.

SIXTEEN

DAY 3

The following morning brought a renewed sense of hope, something the people of Western New York desperately needed. By seven-thirty most heard the breaking news of the overnight events.

"I'm Melissa Holmes, and this is Channel Two Daybreak. Our top stories today include the Army Corps of Engineers beginning examinations of structures along Lake Erie and Buffalo's waterfront for damage from the Scheie wave, pending disaster aid from New York state and the federal government for business and property owners, and Segel International, possibly bringing more divisions and jobs to the Western New York area. But first, we have breaking news that came in overnight; four members of the Trax street gang were arrested for attempted car theft in the parking structure alongside the First Niagara Center. The street gang members were arrested by Buffalo police, but according to reports they were stopped by a super powered metahuman. Channel Two has exclusive footage of night security cameras from the First Niagara Center. We advise some of the footage maybe too graphic for younger viewers."

During the airing of the footage, Holmes provided a blow-by-blow account of the events as they unfolded.

Security camera footage from the parking ramp showed a sharp, black-and-white image of what happened. The Trax became aware of the newcomer, who, after a moment of talking to them, pointed a finger at the one who seemed to be in charge. Then the stranger ran at and leapt at the two closest to him. The stranger, whose back was to the camera, picked up one member with his left hand, raising him off the ground. As his partner tried to sneak up on the stranger, he spun and backhanded the second Trax member with his fist hard enough to send the criminal flying. Then the outsider threw the first man, who had been squirming the whole time, into his partner.

The stranger ran in a direction off-screen. A moment later, a third gang member ran back the way everyone had come, turned, and watched for a moment what was happening off-screen. He fumbled, pulling a handgun from his jacket, aimed, and fired. A second later, the stranger landed on top of the Trax member, grabbing his gun hand and holding him with his left hand, while clutching the man's hand and pulling him closer. Then he dropped the Trax member, who fell to his knees, grasping his hand in what looked like agony, and pieces of the gun fell to the ground. This is where the footage stopped.

Holmes wrapped up the story:

"Sources have confirmed that all gang members were appre-
hended on site, secured by an unknown party. Buffalo police
officers, stationed at the emergency camp at Perry and
Michigan Streets, were contacted by members of the teen
hero group, the New Era, who alerted authorities. Police
spokesman Mike DeGeorge has stated that there is no
comment at this time, but the Buffalo Police Department
will be conducting a thorough investigation into the matter."

As he finished dressing, Alex watched the footage.
Without realizing it, his legs went slack, and he sat on the
edge of his bed, mesmerized by what he had done the night
before. For a minute, he thought it was somebody else. *There
were plenty of metas around, still watching over the waterfront
and downtown,* was the first rational thought he had when he
came out of his trance. Then it hit him like a jolting slap to
the face, and his stomach felt as if it had suddenly filled with
battery acid. Then the memories raced through Alex's mind
like a blinding downpour, unstoppable and overwhelming.
Everything came back in a flash; like a tidal wave flooding
Alex's mind of what happened in the parking structure.

Alex made quick work of the Trax, then hog tied three of
them to a wrought iron fence across the street from the
parking ramp. Being unconscious, he placed them face
down with their hands between the bars then used their
belts to tie them to the fence. The fourth gang member had
his hands and wrists tied to the railing of the adjacent
building and was allowed to sit on the two steps that led
into the building.

8-Ball, who had been sitting on the stoop, surrendered to
Alex in the parking structure after witnessing Alex take
down his three accomplices. In recognition, Alex allowed 8-
Ball to surrender with dignity, avoiding leaving him bound

on the street. Before seeking the police, Alex told 8-Ball, "Get out of this life and do something positive with it. I'm here now, and the Trax are on my radar. If they cross me, I will stop them." Alex then ran nearly two hundred and fifty yards to the end of the block in about ten seconds.

At the end of the street, Alex stood across from the encampment, observing city workers, volunteers, and law enforcement personnel. He paused, trying to figure out what to say, when he noticed a bolt of lightning out of the corner of his eye. Alex saw white crackling bolts of energy streak upward diagonally, and realized it wasn't normal lightning, because it turned in midair, then aimed for the camp. Even without his eagle vision, Alex knew it was the Charger, one of the members of the team of teenage heroes, the New Era. Following the Charger was the female, fire-breathing, demonic Blue Devil. A circular flying platform carried the patriotic Red Raider and the Engineer. Alex walked into the middle of the street, looking up at the quartet of heroes, hoping to catch their attention. If that didn't work, he would head to the police officers, but once he saw the New Era, he reconsidered.

Alex waved his arms frantically and was able to grab their attention, and the Engineer steered his flying platform down towards Alex, followed by the Blue Devil and the Charger. Once on the ground, Alex quickly explained that the Trax were tied up after they tried to steal some of the cars in the parking structure. The Red Raider ordered Charger and the Blue Devil to check out the scene, and the Engineer to use his tech modules, attached to his costume to check the security cameras. As he mentally converted a module into something that tapped into the cameras' systems, Red Raider asked Alex questions.

"Let's just say I'm a concerned citizen and a friend, and we'll leave it at that," Alex said before sprinting down Illinois Street. He moved so quickly that the teenage heroes couldn't react. Reaching the end of the block, Alex jumped into his car, started it up, and sped away as fast as possible.

Red Raider was stunned by Alex's speed, and all Charger and Blue Devil could do was look up from the Trax.

SEVENTEEN

It was just after nine when Marie called Alex back. "Good morning. I didn't expect to hear from you until next week. Sorry I didn't get back to you sooner. My manager told me to take the next few days to recuperate. A girlfriend from work took me out for a spa day yesterday after what happened. Is there a problem?" Alex then heard her say, "Alexia, lower volume," then she said, "Luckily, the bump I took yesterday isn't anything serious, but my bosses are being cautious with everyone who was downtown."

Jumping in, Alex said, "Yeah, makes sense. Even if you're not hurt, there's always the possibility you're still rattled, even if you don't feel it. I'm sorry to bother you, especially after yesterday, but I gotta ask you, have you actually seen any information from my files?" The distress in Alex's voice was impossible to miss.

"I haven't seen any of your records or documents yet, why?"

Under his breath, Alex swore, "Damn," then explained what went down earlier. "I had a visit yesterday from a man named Nick Wolfhart. He says he's my grandfather, and my mother, his daughter, is Ojistah Wolfhart." After a brief sigh, Alex got to the heart of the conversation, "I was hoping you could confirm his story."

Marie's noticeable gasp told Alex this news was a shock to her. "Do you know what he wants?"

After letting out another drawn-out sigh, Alex said, "That's a bit more complicated." He was back in his study, sitting in his broad leather recliner, with his cell in his left hand and his right holding his head, he tried to gather his thoughts.

"How so?" Marie asked.

Alex wasn't prepared to answer that, but he knew she was going to ask him when he called her. "For right now, I can't tell you, it's sort of a confidential family matter, and I don't have the whole picture yet. But once I do, I'll tell you everything. Please believe me, Marie."

For a moment, Marie felt snubbed. "Why not? It's not like you can't trust me." Alex could hear the distress in her voice. Taking a moment to compose herself, Marie said, "Of course I do." She trusted Alex more and more.

Before hanging up, Marie told Alex something straight from the heart. "I want you to promise me something."

"What's that?"

"Be careful. I'm sure I don't have to tell you this, but I wouldn't take anything at face value. I know you said Wolfhart had documents proving everything, and I'm not saying he's a fraud, but someone appearing unexpectedly like this, especially with the timing of your files being released, seems too coincidental. There have been a few cases where so-called family members came out of nowhere, looking to reconnect, but those usually involved some kind of inheritance or money."

"Yeah, I know what you're saying, and I've already disregarded the idea. I'm not in line for anything like that, and he offered proof that can't be explained. It's part of what I'll make clear later." Alex took a step further out on that limb. "Right now, all I can tell you is it's connected to a couple of local metahumans, Wildrun and the Red Warrior."

"What?" Marie asked.

Alex couldn't miss the fascination in Marie's voice.

"Like I said, I don't know all the details yet, but I'm meeting with Wolfhart later this morning to get the whole story. The only other thing I can tell you is I'm connected to them as well."

"I'm not familiar with those names."

"They were a couple of heroes around here. The Red Warrior was active in the forties and fifties, and Wildrun during the sixties."

"What do you think it all means?"

Alex knew but decided to keep quiet for the time being. After speaking with Grandmother, Marie would have carte blanche. He hated himself for lying to Marie, but he knew he didn't have a choice at this point. All he could say was, "Right now, I don't have the damnedest idea."

———

Alex stepped outside onto a damp cement patio, which told him it briefly rained overnight, but now he was forced to squint his eyes due to the sun blinding him. As he walked down the driveway alongside his parents' cars, he found the air fresh and clear.

The somber rain clouds had finally departed overnight, and the sun was shining for the first time in what felt like ages. The sky was a bright and bold shade of blue, with white clouds that looked like bundles of cotton.

Alex took off without talking to his parents, unsure of what to say about the previous night's events. He figured that, eventually, they would find out, then question him before scolding him thoroughly. For now, he needed to meet Wolfhart and tell him exactly what was on his mind.

Despite everything Alex tried to process everything that was happening, which wasn't easy. The only thing he was positive of was Alex didn't want this responsibility, and he was intent on telling Wolfhart and this Grandmother exactly what he thought.

As he drove south, away from the city, the memory of tapping into his animalistic abilities came back to him. Alex had to be honest and silently admitted, he loved the rush of it all. It made him smile.

Ever since he was a boy Alex dreamt of what it'd be like to have super strength or be able to fly like in the comic books he used to collect. To actually be one of the real-life metahumans, the idea was overwhelming and enticing at the same time.

Alex quickly realized something as he made his way through Lackawanna into Blasdell; he realized that he loved the rush and the power he felt when he fought the Trax. He loved being to out muscle them and run the length of a city block in ten seconds. He knew the sensory overload was something he knew he get used to.

———

It took Alex over forty minutes to reach the Cattaraugus Reservation driving Route 5, also known as Lake Shore Drive. As he passed through the towns and villages along the lake shore, he saw firsthand the wreckage left in the seiche's wake. He realized that mostly innocent people were affected, with lakefront homes and businesses suffering damage from the wave. At one point, he saw children helping their parents with the cleanup. Alex felt as though his stomach had a hole in it, imploding in the middle. Suddenly, everything became clear.

Alex reached the town of Farnham, with open farmland on his right and vibrant, autumn-colored forests on his left, all exploding with peak foliage colors. As he passed a huge gas station/store at the entrance of the reservation, he finally admitted to himself that he was scared. He had put on a brave front for everyone, not letting his parents know how he truly felt, but deep down, Alex was downright terrified. He didn't want anyone to worry, but he knew it might be impossible to hide.

Just before the turnoff to Maiden Lane Road, Alex found Wolfhart's cabin and pulled into the gravel driveway, spotting Dorset's SUV. "Great," he said, somehow making the simple word sound like an F-bomb.

The crisp fall air carried a hint of woodsmoke, and the mid-morning sun cast a golden glow on the vibrant foliage. Despite it being Alex's favorite weather and season, he didn't feel any better as he walked up the three short steps onto the cabin's front porch. After knocking on the front door, he looked over the two-story wooden structure and thought *Not too bad.*

Alex watched as Wolfhart opened the door, which creaked loudly, announcing to everyone that the hinges needed oil. "Good morning, did you find the cabin okay?" Wolfhart asked with a broad smile, as if Alex were there for a casual visit. Both men knew that was far from the truth.

Since Alex was emotionally transparent, he couldn't hide anything from Wolfhart. He stood there, reminiscent of how Wyatt Earp might have stood at the O.K. Corral. For an uncomfortable moment, neither said a word, then finally Alex said, "Yeah, your directions were fine."

"Come in," Wolfhart said playing the host. Then he

asked, "Feeling all right, I mean you're not too tired or sore?"

As Alex came inside, he instantly detected the scent of coffee hanging in the air and said, "No I'm fine."

Alex followed Wolfhart towards the kitchen, and as they made their way through the living room, Alex glanced around at the laid-back but comfortable cabin, and thought it had nice feminine touches, which Alex attributed to his grandmother, then noticed the photos on the mantle. Instinctively he stared at them, scanning for one face in particular.

"Good, glad to hear it, especially after your busy night with the Trax."

Oh boy, Alex thought.

"Yeah, I saw the news, not quite what I expected," Wolfhart said, then Alex noticed a slight frown on Wolfhart's face, and the elderly man had trouble looking Alex in the eyes.

Alex began to realize a couple of things: First, Wolfhart was legit, but this was something he had already figured out before tapping into the strength of the bear. Secondly, Alex realized that Wolfhart was expecting more from his grandson than someone who was merely showing off, like a teenager who just got his driver's license and "borrowed" his father's classic sports car to impress his friends. "I knew you'd be in the public eye sooner or later, but I didn't think it'd happen so fast."

They joined Orsen, who was sitting at the kitchen island, drinking coffee and greeted Alex with a simple "Morning".

Wolfhart offered Alex a cup, but Alex shook his head, just saying no thanks. To be frank, he'd rather drink diesel fuel and breathe into a campfire, coffee was not his drink of choice in the morning. After experiencing the waterfront, he was glad he didn't have his wolf's nose right now. Wolfhart sat down at the counter, gesturing for Alex to join him, and poured half a cup of coffee for himself.

The nervous energy and tension that had been building up suddenly evaporated as Alex tried to explain things. "You gotta believe I didn't plan on all that. I just went out last night to clear my head, found myself downtown, and it was a case of right time, wrong place, I guess. Nobody was around, no cops or any of the heroes, and something inside me told me, no, ordered me to stop them. I can't explain it or make myself clearer."

Alex saw that both men were listening intently. Finally, Wolfhart spoke, "I'm not discounting what you're saying happened, but you're going to have to be extremely careful."

"What do you mean?" Alex asked.

Wolfhart placed his mug on the counter and emphasized his point by extending his worn and hardened hands towards Alex. "Your mission is to protect the planet and life, both human and animal, when and where needed. But if you make enemies, it could add to the danger. Believe me, this is something I know too well. I first put on the mask because, back in the day, others had started wearing them for several reasons—either to maintain some privacy or to protect their families, which eventually became a priority for me.

"Now what you're telling me I never experienced, hopefully Grandmother will have some answers for us."

"Speaking of which, do you have any idea what I have to do? I mean, what's going to happen when we get to wherever we're going?"

Wolfhart shook his head. "Honestly, I don't know myself. All I can tell you is Grandmother will know."

Alex felt his confusion and angst rising. "Tell me about her. She's not my actual grandmother, right?"

Wolfhart would have spit out coffee in that moment if

he'd been drinking and began laughing. "Oh lord no! We're not related to her, at least not in a traditional sense. Grandmother is our people's healer and spiritual leader, but she's so much more."

"What do you mean?"

Wolfhart explained as best he could. "No one knows how old she really is, but she has been watching over our people for an exceedingly long time. She is in touch with the Great Spirit to levels most cannot comprehend."

After taking a swallow of his coffee, Wolfhart continued, "All I'm positive of is Grandmother is a woman of great power, how powerful I don't know, but we know there have been and are others like Lady Victory from the first group of Guardsmen or Tarot from the Midway, among others, but Grandmother is more, like I said she's a spiritual leader, and wise, but you'll see for yourself Alex." After finishing his coffee, Wolfhart asked, "Ready?"

The pressure had been building, and Alex reached his limit. Standing there, glancing down, Alex let out a sigh, then shook his head. "No not really. I mean you come to me with this whole story and tell me I'm supposed to be some world saver. You have any goddamned idea how screwed up this? I'm just some guy from Buffalo, I'm no hero, I can't do this. It's too much for me."

"Alex", Wolfhart said, placing his hand on Alex's shoulder, "I understand this is a lot for you to take in and yes, it's not fair to slam you with this out of the blue the way I did. In a way I'd been dreading meeting you all my life because I knew I'd have to tell you that you'd have to carry this load. It's not fair to ask anyone to bare this sort of responsibility."

Orsen just stood there listening in a sad silence. Alex was being told he had to place his life on hold, possibly forget any future plans he had, maybe forget the idea of a normal life, a family, because of risking his own life. He might not be there for them. There were men and women who did this daily, most without powers or abilities, but for the majority it was a vocation. That wasn't the case here.

Wolfhart continued. "If I could, I'd take this all back, but I can't." He stopped and placed his hand on Alex's right shoulder. "You're my grandson, and I know we just met, and we don't know each other, but I'm hoping in time we will. I don't know why it has to be you, but no matter what happens I'm here for you as much as I know your family are there for you too."

Finally, Orsen spoke up in his gravelly voice. "Ah, Alex I'm not good at this sorta thing, I know we didn't get off on the right foot, and I know this is a lot for you to grasp, but I've known your granddad a long time, and he's as solid as they come." Extending his hand, he added, 'Let's start over."

Alex let everything sink in and finally he smiled and shook Orsen's hand. "Glad to know you."

"Good, now that that's over," Wolfhart went on, "We have to get going."

"Want me to come along?" Orsen asked.

"I would but you can't, old buddy. Sorry."

Orsen stood there a little disappointed, but Alex noticed he respected Wolfhart's wishes. "Is there anything I can do?"

Wolfhart just shook his head, "Not really, just keep good thoughts for us, and wish us luck."

Orsen looked back to Alex. "Good luck. If you guys need anything, call my cell. I'll be here just in case." To cut the tension he said, "Actually it's a good thing I can't go, since there's a football match I'm anxious to see, and I can catch here on your flat screen. Manchester United's playing Sheffield. At least I can see the whole game." He cracked a wide smile.

Wolfhart just shook his head letting out a chuckle, "Fine just leave some beers this time."

"Nah, mate, it's too early in the day. 'Sides that lite beer you buy, runs right through me. Next time have some proper English Ale on hand," he shot back.

As Alex and Wolfhart got into Alex's car Orsen watched them knowing Wolfhart was a capable man, and Alex seemed like he'd be capable of keeping it together, but had a feeling something really bad was coming around the bend, like a freight train and none of them could do anything to get out of its path.

———

As Alex drove, following Wolfhart's directions to Grandmother's dwelling, he tried to describe to Alex will be capable of, if worthy. "As strong as you are now, your body, mind, and spirit will reach levels you can't imagine. I can't tell you how exactly, but you'll be connected to the Earth, even more so than you are now. You're linked to the physical, animalistic powers, as formidable as they are, they're nothing compared to what you'll be capable of. These abilities will be among your strongest gifts."

"What do you mean?" Alex kept an eye on where he was headed.

Wolfhart looked solemn. "Honestly, I don't know. According to Grandmother what's coming has to do with the spiritual, sacred side of your abilities, which no other family member could gain, or manage. It'll take more strength than you can imagine to maintaining control."

Alex felt a constant sense of anxiety, like he was about to snap and Wolfhart's words nearly pushed him over the edge, but what he said next was a lifeline for Alex. "Thanks to Orsen, I think you're capable, that's why I had him tailing you, I had to be sure of your character. Of course you'll have a lot of support, there's your parents, there's me and Orsen, Grandmother will be there for you, and I'm sure you've got other friends."

Alex instantly thought of Marie and knew he could count on her, but he didn't know what to think about her since all thoughts vanished from his mind which left him in a fog.

After an uncomfortable silence, Alex finally asked the question that had sporadically occupied his thoughts since he was five years old but had dominated his mind for the past eighteen hours. With a sad expression, he asked "What can you tell me about my mother?"

It was only natural for Alex to be curious, that's what made him go to Homeward Angels in the first place, and it finally occurred to Wolfhart, so for the rest of the trip he told Alex all he could about Ojistah.

"Well, when your mother was five years old, I realized she was born with a true spirit. We had a huge oak tree in front of our yard, and she was determined to climb it as high as she could. She tried and fell more than once. One time, she broke her right arm. Even though she cried out loud when she landed, Ojistah never let on how bad she was hurt after that. I'll tell you something: the afternoon her cast was cut off, she was out there again. Your mother climbed that tree and made it all the way."

Alex saw the pride in Wolfhart's face; his smile was a dead giveaway. But he shifted gears to the one question that had been foremost in his mind since Wolfhart appeared. "What happened? I mean, why'd she disappear? I know what you said yesterday, but there's got to be more to it."

The mood quickly shifted from lighthearted to solemn. "All I can tell you is what I told you before. When she came to me and told me she was pregnant, I didn't take the news well. We argued, it got really ugly, I said things I'm not proud of. Ojistah stormed out, and that was the last I saw of her."

Alex wasn't sure what to say as they drove on in an uncomfortable, awkward silence. Finally, Alex broke the difficult quiet. "I've got to be honest. Ever since I was little, for some reason, and don't ask me why, I always felt like it was my fault. Maybe if I hadn't come into the picture…" Alex couldn't finish what he was saying, but his point was made.

"No, no, don't think that way," Wolfhart practically begged. "What happened between your mother and me was solely my fault. Don't ever think this was your fault. I'm positive your parents would agree with me a hundred percent."

———

They talked as they made their way down Main Street, over the snaking Cattaraugus Creek, away from the heart of the reservation. Then somewhere before the neighboring farms, Alex turned onto a dirt road, when Wolfhart told him to turn, which took them into a heavily forested area.

The Charger began bouncing up and down, and Alex hoped he wasn't tearing up his undercarriage or break line as Wolfhart just smiled and said, "Grandmother lives majorly off the grid." Alex just glanced at him, trying to keep an eye on the "road".

Finally, they slowed to a dead stop, because the road trickled down to a dry muddy path. Wolfhart got out. "We're here."

Alex looked around and was confused. There were no houses or buildings and was about to ask Wolfhart if he was positive, but then he saw the dirt road dead ended. The 'road' dwindled down to a narrow foot path. "This way," Wolfhart said.

Alex followed Wolfhart along the trail, into the wooded area about two hundred yards. Eventually they reached a small clearing, where Alex saw a longhouse just sitting there, on its own. The shelter, with its wooden frame cloaked in bark and moss, stretched over twenty feet in length and nine feet in width, standing majestically at just over ten feet tall. It exuded an ancient, almost magical charm, like a gateway to a forgotten forest realm.

"What is it?" Alex asked.

"A longhouse," Wolfhart answered. "A traditional Iroquois shelter for several families. There's a central aisle, with sections, down along each side, at the ends are storage compartments, with hearths and smoke holes in the roof. Normally two families shared a hearth and each longhouse would house several generations of an extended family. Ever see anything like it?"

Alex slowly shook his head, "I had no idea. So, no teepees for you guys, huh," Alex sarcastically joked, which from Wolfhart's expression, took offense to.

He stepped right up to Alex, placing his hand on his grandson's barrel chest, stopping Alex mid-step. "Don't make those kinds of jokes around here. You are my grand-son, and your bloodline traces to your mother, but you don't know shit about your family or our traditions, or your heritage. There are plenty of residents on the reservation who wouldn't understand what's happening, let alone welcome you. Your skins too fair, you've been raised in the 'white man's world', and I can think of several who'd be willing to call you Half-Breed, or not just say worse, but try to do worse. Show some damn respect."

Alex took the message to heart and just said "Yes, sir," and meant it.

As they got closer, Alex finally saw an elderly woman sitting on a simple bench made of logs and cut wood, seemingly meditating. She appeared to be decades older than Wolfhart, and Alex couldn't fathom her exact age. He knew Wolfhart was slightly older than Reggie, placing him in his eighties.

Before the Medicine Woman lay a circle of stones, bearing signs of past fires. Alex guessed it was for something sacred. "Grandmother," Wolfhart said, smiling as he gestured toward Alex, who was a couple steps behind, "Let me introduce my grandson, Alexander Harlow."

Alex was surprised at how quickly she rose up, with the aid of her staff, that was a sturdy piece of weathered wood, rough and unpolished, showcasing its natural curves and knots. Three eagle feathers were bound at the top with strips of worn leather, their tips fluttering in the breeze. The entire staff seemed like it had been part of the forest for centuries, embodying the spirit of the wilderness.

"I've been expecting you my sons." She approached Alex, looking him square in the face. Before he could speak, Grandmother raised her weathered, copper hand to his face. "I know you have many questions and fears, my son. They will be answered in time, but time is running like a coursing river. It rushes past us, and we must hurry to reach our destination." She ran her hand down to Alex's chest, placing it over the mark Shunkaha Wakinyan left on him, then locked eyes with him.

Instinctively, Alex knew she was aware of what had happened. "Yes, my son," she quietly said, a smile crossing her weathered face. "I know you have your concerns, Alexander. They will be addressed, I promise." The sage placed her hand on Alex's chest, over his heart. "I know you are scared, which is understandable. But before we go, know this: you are stronger than you realize. Time is critical now, and we must go." She emphasized her point by driving the bottom of her staff into the ground, making a divot in the dirt.

More confused now than before Alex started to look around and do a double take, "What, I thought this whatever was here."

Grandmother shook her head. "No, child, I must first guide you to the Sanctuary, and there, we will find the answers you seek." With those words, she turned and began walking toward the longhouse. Upon nearly reaching it, she headed to the left to go around and behind it. Without question, Wolfhart followed her, almost obediently.

Alex, more confused than ever, realized he wasn't going to get any answers at that moment. He knew there was only one thing to do—go to the Sanctuary.

EIGHTEEN

Segel and Macaria left later than normal since his meeting the Senecan leaders was set for late morning. When he joined Macaria in the SUV he said, "I want to be there early, do you know how to get to the reservation," already knowing what her answer was going to be.

"Absolutely," Macaria replied. "I looked up the fastest route to Irving last night," she added as she slid the seat belt over her shoulder and clicked it in place.

"Good," he said as he settled in the backseat, but instead of reading the news on his tablet, Segel reviewed his proposal one final time. The man had finished by the time they reached the Main Street entrance to the 290-90 interchange and thought to himself as he looked at his reflection on his tablet's screen.

You know what you're doing. This is just another acquisition; you've done fifty of them and haven't lost one.

———

After reviewing his proposal for a final time, Segel relaxed by reading the morning news on his tablet like normal. What wasn't normal was the lead story.

Dumbfounded couldn't begin to describe how Segel felt as he read the feature story. "What the hell...." was the only thing he could mutter out.

Macaria sensed something was wrong. She tore through the maze of thruways and interstates, skillfully bobbing and weaving through Northtown's late morning traffic. Despite the congestion, she made excellent time traveling from Amherst to Hamburg, having missed the morning rush hour. "What's wrong?" Macaria asked as she maneuvered through the roads, cutting off a slow-moving cargo van before accelerating along Route 5, quickly passing the Ford Stamping plant in Woodlawn.

"Ah nothing," he uncharacteristically said back.

In that moment Macaria knew something wasn't right. Not having the typical employer/employee relationship Macaria got away with a plethora other employers wouldn't tolerate, including calling her boss names. "Bullshitter," she muttered.

"What?" Segel asked coming out his mesmerized state, then it hit him like a slap to the back of the head, "What did you say?" He looked up from his tablet.

Giving the occasional glance in the rear-view mirror into Segel's dark eyes because she had to keep her eyes on the traffic, Macaria said, "You heard me, something's got you spooked. I can see it."

Segel knew he couldn't fool his confidante, recounted the article he had read, suspicious at the timing. "According to the Buffalo News, last night four members of that street gang, the Trax, were arrested for attempted car theft downtown."

"Points for ambition and seizing an opportunity, but

Christ, ransacking disaster victims. These assholes oughta get worked over so much they'll beg for someone to do them."

"Just remember they were only attempting to steal cars; it's not like they were involved in human trafficking or child molestation. This is the interesting part, I quote the article, "According to authorities the gang members were captured single handedly, by a super-powered human, possessing enormous physical strength and speed. Security footage obtained at the scene showed this unidentified metahuman snatching a gun from one of the Trax members, then destroyed it. Afterwards the unknown party took care of the delinquents, then contacted members of the New Era, and ran off at blinding speed. It's estimated he was running nearly thirty miles per hour."

Fascinated, Macaria only said, "Well that's something," as she changed lanes, while keeping pace at almost sixty miles per hour.

"Yeah something," was Segel's only answer.

"Wait a second," Macaria said realizing what was running through Segel's mind. "I know what you're think-ing, and you said it yourself when you told me about the Calcite, there's a lot of supers running around." Trying to reassure Segel, Macaria added, "Just cause this guy shows up last night, stomps those bangers, that doesn't mean anything with your plans. The timing's just coincidence."

After letting out a sigh, Segel sat, listening to Macaria's words. He wanted to feel more confident because he knew she was right, but experience taught him not to make such assumptions. Over the years, Segel set up special 'deals' four times, all handled by intermediaries, removed three or four levels from him. These deals were all thwarted by heroes on the West Coast, Russia, and Canada. Despite being so far removed from the principal players and remaining untouchable in these transactions, Segel didn't feel any better for some reason.

"Perhaps," was Segel's only response as the BMW approached the town of Wanakah. As the pair continued southbound towards the reservation, Segel stared out at the now calm waters of Lake Erie, suddenly overwhelmed with an uncomfortable feeling. The timing of everything happening in such a short window made Segel feel like a perfect storm was coming. Not that he'd admit it, but for a man who needed to maintain control, this was not good.

Segel pulled his phone from his inside pocket, brought up his contacts, and scrolled to the J's until he found the name he was looking for. "Jacob, I have a job for you. I need you at the Cattaraugus Reservation."

NINETEEN

Alex followed behind the two elders on the footpath and quickly realized Wolfhart already knew their destination. "What's this Sanctuary you're talking about?" It was then he noticed Grandmother walked a bit slower than he and Wolfhart were. Naturally, Alex assumed it was due to her advanced age.

She used her staff for support, as she climbed a slight incline, and her breathing seemed a little labored. Alex was about to offer his assistance when she addressed his concerns, before he could say anything.

"Do not worry about me my son, I am fine. It occurs when one becomes middle-aged." She turned back slightly, towards a startled Alex.

Wolfhart just laughed, knowing Grandmother's abilities were not to be underestimated, even at her advanced age.

Grandmother continued, "The Sanctuary is a site untouched by man, where those who believe in the native ways, Nature's path, can come to reflect, rest, gather their strength for the paths that lie ahead of them."

As they went on, Alex realized the longhouse vanished,

almost as if it were swallowed up by the forest. Suddenly a chilling fog rose out of nowhere and Alex knew this wasn't right, because the weather conditions weren't right for fog. But he reminded himself he was dealing with phenomena beyond those of mortal men, and inexplicably, Shakespeare's *Hamlet* came to mind.

As they continued, the fog lifted, and once Alex's vision cleared, he saw Grandmother had led them into a clearing surrounded by heavy forest. Ahead of them was a crackling campfire, set in a circle of stones. Outside the circle, were four wooden stumps, and further outside from the second ring were logs that could seat two to three people. Shrubs and bushes, plants, and some young saplings grew about the grounds, and about twenty-five yards away from the fire circle was a small, self-contained body of water, and as captivating as the grounds were, the one thing that captured Alex's attention was that there was a diverse assortment of animals scattered about the Sanctuary. Rabbit, skunk, brown bear, various species of birds, robins and sparrows, to falcons, hawks, and even a bald eagle. But what astonished Alex the most was that the predators were coexisting in harmony with their usual prey.

"What is...." the words trailed off because Alex couldn't find the words to describe what was racing through his mind.

Grandmother simply said, "This place is for gathering one's strength, both physical and mental, for animal and men alike," then with her withered hand Grandmother gestured towards one of the larger logs, indicating she wanted the men to sit. Wolfhart immediately sat down, Alex followed, a little slower because he was taking everything in.

Grandmother began rummaging through the pouch she wore on her belt and told Alex a story he never could have imagined in his wildest dreams. "Eons ago, when the world was new, the Great Spirit knew Grandmother Earth would need guardians, protectors." Then she pulled a violet/blueish powder that sparkled from her pouch and threw it into the fire. Once the fine particles contacted the flames there was a small explosion of smoke and light, and the existing fire turned green.

As Grandmother spoke, she waved her staff over the rising flames, and suddenly images of those she spoke about rose out of the smoke. "These sentinels are considered myth and legend, have been called the Primal Guardians, but eventually as men began to explore the world, they encountered the offspring, and gave them names such as Sasquatch, Thunderbird, Yeti, and Kraken, among others. The Great Spirit knew they would not be enough.

At seeing the visions, Alex felt his jaw go slack.

"Eventually the Great Spirit spoke to a young woman, who was among our people, telling her of the inevitable dangers that would come, and how she would be needed, much the way you are. The Great Spirit unlocked the power in her mind and body, revealing answers to questions this child never dreamt existed, from that day she was known as Ghost Dancer.

Alex 'saw' a beautiful, light-copper toned woman, with dark brown eyes, and jet-black hair that ran all the way down her back. She wore an off the shoulder deer skin dress, bejeweled with porcupine quills, beads, and silver brooches. Ghost Dancer also wore a something that resembled a tiara, that looked like it was made of deer antler, animal bones, and wood, with a bright blue gem in the center of her headdress.

"The Great Spirit instructed Ghost Dancer to gather individuals, each endowed with great power or skill, to defend all the Nations from various threats, both native and foreign invaders. For nearly ten centuries, these men and women united to combat evil and the myriad dangers that threatened not only our people but all Nations. Over time, they became known to both friend and foe as the Wolf Clan of the Longhouse."

The visions shifted, revealing Ghost Dancer and her allies to Alex. Tatanka Wicahpi (Star of the Running Deer), who could run faster than her namesake; Wiyaka Hota (Feather of the Night Hawk), gifted with flight; Wakinyan Itazipa (Thunder Bow), a born tracker and hunter who never missed with his bow and arrows; Hoksila Mahpiya (Boy of the Sky), who commanded the winds; Iya Wakan (Sacred Rain) who summoned storms and the rains, Taha Ska (White Turtle) who possessed great strength and was invulnerable.

The visions then shifted to the threats as Grandmother spoke their names: Tsithunva (Snake Dancer), a dangerous witch of the Hopi; Ursa and her allies, the Man Bear Tribe from far up north; the monstrous Skinwalkers; Pahosca Wapaha (Bloodcrow) a dark mage; and the Viking invaders from Scandinavia, Þöröx and his raiders.

Alex recalled hearing about some of these individuals on a History Channel series about the metahuman history of North America.

Grandmother continued, "Soon after an Iroquois warrior named Gah-noh-dah-oh, translated as Iron Wolf received a vision that showed him the changes that would occur to his peoples' way of life. To protect their existence, Iron Wolf prayed to Hiawatha for guidance and aid. We believe he walks in the Land of the Spirits, where he and others watch over and guide our destinies. Hiawatha opened Iron Wolf's mind to use the power in his body and mind that went untouched, and then decreed that Iron Wolf's descendants, such as your mother and grandfather, would be the guardians of the Earth until a time came when the Earth would need a guardian more powerful than any. This custodian of the planet would master the fires that burn, the waters that flow and provide life, the land that provides, and the winds that move the storms and rain showers. Each element would respond to their will when needed. Alexander Harlow, you are that guardian, you are the Rainbow Warrior."

The images shifted as Grandmother spoke, they grew darker and grim. "After the white man arrived on this continent there would be no stopping the tide that was coming, and the Great Spirit and The Sacred Circle knew men would exploit the land and water, poison the air, hunt animal life for their own greed, stupidity, and arrogance, some to the point of extinction, so other guardians were called upon. Some were granted powers beyond mortal men, others rose of their accord, but they rose to do what was right and just, but your family were destined to be the true caretakers of Grandmother Earth."

Alex shook off the images and said "Look, he," indicating Wolfhart, "Already gave me the sales pitch, and I admit yeah there is something because of these powers I have, but I'm no world saver. I'm just a guy who's barely making it by. My ex dumped me last year, I've been in one shitty, dead-end job after another, and the only reason I've been able to come out here is cause my office is closed for the time being, and now you're throwing all this at me." In total defiance Alex drew his line in the sand. "I'm not saying there isn't something here, after last night and seeing those images or whatever there were, but you can't make this my responsibility. It's not fair or right. I didn't ask or want it." Alex got up to leave and Wolfhart tried to stop him.

Alex was taking the arrowhead off his neck when Grandmother used her staff to swat at Alex's hand, without hurting him. "Alexander you are correct, you did not ask this destiny, and it is not fair to make this responsibility yours."

Wolfhart acknowledged Alex's feelings but supported Grandmother. "She's right. It's not fair to drop this on you now. Some of those superhumans have been training since childhood and been preparing themselves their whole lives. But believe me Alex, if I could, I'd take this burden from you. I wouldn't want this responsibility normally, but you're my grandson. I'd do what's required, but the truth is, I can't. No one else can do this. You're the one."

"Your grandfather is correct," Grandmother added. "You are born of both the Red Man and the White Man, a living unification of man, a living example of the unification Grandmother Earth will have with mankind in time."

Then Grandmother took her Medicine Pouch that hung from her neck and poured a handful of a sparkling gray/black powder out into her left palm. "Now my child is the time for you to convene with your Spirit Guides." Then she suddenly blew the powder into Alex's face, and he inhaled.

———

Alex noticed a strong, flowery aroma to the powder, then without warning his mind was transported to another domain.

He stood like a bronze statue in a park, but his mind ascended to a plane of existence few men ever reached without dying. He was back where he faced Shunkaha Wakinyan. His thoughts cleared, his breathing slowed, and his heart rate decreased. Here, Alex Harlow would be granted the powers his mind and spirit needed to match those of his body.

Alex realized there was order and serenity here; he felt it, as his 'third eye' saw beyond the clouds, into the stars, rocketing with an unparalleled speed to the 'Pillars of Creation.' There, Alex learned the truth of the colossal cosmic entity's fingers and hand. Alex's spirit reached out for the entity as if his body were present. Suddenly, he turned earthward. Alex built speed, feeling both pulled and propelled toward Earth. As he pierced the upper atmosphere, a mass of black and grey clouds lit up like a thunderstorm.

Once through the clouds, Alex saw a distant mountain range with snowcapped peaks and mist-filled valleys. In the distance, he noticed two structures. The first was a sheer tower of rock and stone, in shades matching the landscape, dwarfing the Burj Khalifa in Dubai. Time and weather had eroded this wonder, and soon, Alex found himself atop it. From this vantage point, he saw the second mass clearly. It marked the beginning of a mountain range of worn-down rock, with a giant eagle feather etched into its face.

Alex looked in amazement as a blueish-white light descended on him. It grew larger as it approached, enveloping him. The crackling energy surrounded him, and he heard what initially sounded like a rumble of thunder. As the sounds drew nearer, Alex realized they were the growls and roars of three or four animals at their fullest fury. One by one, they emerged and surrounded him, letting Alex know he would never be alone again.

First came the eagle, chief of the skies and servant of the sun, granting Alex clear vision and a pure spirit. Next, the cougar leapt towards Alex, showing leadership, power, courage, and balance. The grizzly bear followed, bringing power, cunning, and healing. A wolf then emerged, demonstrating loyalty, perseverance, and stability. Finally, the Great White Buffalo approached Alex. As they stood face to face, looking into each other's eyes, she provided curing powers and strengths he'd never known before.

The animals formed a circle around Alex and when completed, they took on a glowing golden aura as their energies flowed into their champion. At this moment, Alex couldn't move or speak, he could barely breathe and felt a lump in his throat the size of a hand grenade. He didn't know what to do, say or think. His mind was totally void of thought. Suddenly he realized he was not alone, when he heard Grandmother chanting.

Alex didn't understand what she was saying, as Grandmother continued to pray, she switched over to English. "High Father Hiawatha, Grandmother Earth, we are here to let this warrior's journey begin, so that he may protect this planet and your children. I beg you and the other Guardians of the Sacred Circle, grant our plea."

The clouds became dark and forbidding, the winds increased and howl stronger than before, and Alex had never seen a storm roll in so quickly. It seemed as if the light of the day itself had begun to vanish, as if it were already dusk. Suddenly a blinding white light burst out of nowhere.

Instinctively bracing for the unknown, Alex's body hummed with blue-white energy, believing himself ready as the light grew blinding.

Grandmother shut her eyes, her prayers in Iroquois rising above the crescendo. The light peaked, searing through him. The overwhelming light and acute sound battered his heightened senses, pushing him to the brink of unconsciousness. Abruptly, the light faded out and died, plunging everything into darkness and silence.

———

Alex opened his eyes, realized he was back in his body, in the real world when he saw Wolfhart standing there. The older man was visibally shaken and concerned.

Grandmother came up to Alex and said, "You have immense potential my child, but you are like a child holding a parent's firearm. You have great power and potential, and the Animal Guides gave you not only their strengths, but the instincts to use your abilities. Although you lack the knowledge needed, although that will come in time, with proper training and guidance."

Slowly, Alex began to comprehend, as if awakening from the fog of sleep. He asked, "Now what?"

Before anyone could answer, from above the Sanctuary a thunderous voice announced, *"That is for another time Alexander Harlow!"* Everyone looked up to see Shunkaha Wakinyan above them with a new, angered look in his predatory eyes.

Grandmother asked, "Why do you say that Shunkaha Wakinyan?"

"Alexander is needed now, to save the Seneca Nation!"

Looking into the deity's eyes high above him, without realizing it Alex's right hand reached for the arrowhead hanging from his neck, because he knew the time was now.

Somehow, Alex instinctively knew where he needed to go and where he was needed. As he triggered his newfound abilities, his body crackled with an unseen energy, and power coursed through him. Fully engaged, Alex saw a mental image of the reservation's government building. He watched a large African American man place a device at a gas meter and activate the bomb. "My God," was all Alex could say.

"Alex what is it?" Wolfhart asked, as he and Grandmother watched in amazement. They saw Alex go into a trance-like state, but they knew there was more to it all.

Alex's eyes had changed shape, appearing more avian, and glowed with bright blueish-white energy, giving him an almost alien appearance.

"A bomb, I think, at a building with three flags in front of it, a sort of circular roof in the center of two other buildings, and the flags are an American flag, a red and white, and a purple and white flag, in front of it."

Alarmed, Wolfhart said, "Jesus, that sounds like the government building here on the reservation! Alex are you positive it's a bomb?"

"I believe so, I can see it's zip tied to a gas meter. There's a pair of lights, one's a blinking green light, and a steady red light." Alex knew immediately he had to act.

Grandmother didn't hesitate, pointing with her staff, as she commanded Alex what to do. "Follow the path back to the longhouse, you will find the main road, take it, run, stop that explosive!"

"What? How?" was his only response.

"There's no time to explain, go now or innocents will die," and, with her last words still hanging in mid-air, Alex did as ordered. He ran like he'd never moved before in his life.

TWENTY

Segel appeared from the government building, looking composed and professional, beneath the surface, he was a volcano, primed to erupt. The man harbored a desire to unleash as much destruction as possible, indifferent to the casualties and chaos that would follow in his wake.

Macaria recognized the look on Segel's face, instantly she knew the proposal was shot down, and it was not good. The muscles in his face were tight, and the ones in his neck throbbed. Segel was accustomed to acquiring whatever he wanted, anytime, anyplace, from anyone. Being told no was a rarity, and Macaria knew that when those rejections happened, bad things ensued. Graveyards around the world held those who had said, "No" to Segel.

Macaria was about to open the driver's door, playing her chauffeur's role to the hilt, but Segel waved her off with his right hand, and opened the door himself. Being the woman she was, Macaria considered poking the bear but thought better of it once she saw the look in Segel's face in the rearview mirror and wisely decided to stay quiet. She just sat and watched him make a call on his cell.

"Where are you?" Then came a pause. "Good. I'm outside. You know what to do. Call me when done." He hung up then ordered, "Don't start the engine, yet."

"All right, I assume the Indians didn't accept your offer, but why are we waiting?" Macaria asked as they watched Jacob pull his dark blue convertible Audi from the right side of the parking lot, near an area in-between the government building and the Seneca Nation of Indians Library. "Jacob's doing his thing, why not leave? He's an expert, this isn't his first time."

"True, but I have two reasons for staying. First, when the future leaders of the Senecas see that building on fire, I want them to know I'm involved. Whether they can prove it or not is another matter, but they will have to take my next offer very seriously. Second, I want to watch that building burn to the ground."

Macaria was taken aback; she had never heard him sound so venomous. Over their fifteen-plus year relationship, she'd seen Segel commit morally questionable acts to blatant criminal actions, but a daytime bombing of the government building was a level he had never reached before. Macaria knew, no matter what happened, this was going to be bad. In that moment she began wondering about looking for an exit.

They watched as Jacob walked around to the left side of the building, then disappeared around the corner. "Now what?" Macaria asked.

"Now," Segel responded while looking through some files from his briefcase, "we wait for Jacob's call."

Macaria turned as best she could to face Segel. "So, what happened in there?"

With a wild look in his eyes, Segel for a moment seemed like he couldn't focus, then after calming down he pulled himself together, and told her what happened. "I spoke with the President, the Executive Assistant, and the Chief of Staff, explained to them about the Caltrate and its value, and that Segel International was willing to pay the residences more than any of the residents could imagine for their properties. I explained we'd approach the government about the deal, to obtain federal approval before the sale could go through, but they refused. Those fools claimed too much had been taken, stolen from their people. Also, it was a matter of protecting their heritage."

"How bad is the blast going be?" Macaria's concerns weren't for the employees or visitors, but a factor no one planned for. During the meeting, Macaria watched as a group of day-schoolers headed into the library for a field trip. Seeing the children made her admit she had certain lines she'd never cross.

"The device is something R&D has been working on, for some interested parties. Once detonated, the blast mimics a gas explosion perfectly."

"No, I mean how large will the blast be?"

"The building will be rubble in less than two minutes, but it shouldn't go any further than that. Why?"

Knowing Segel was slightly paranoid, despite their relationship, Macaria quickly covered herself, because she didn't want to show any sign of weakness. "Just curious."

Segel's phone rang before anyone could say another word. "Yes?" Segel paused, then they saw Jacob coming from along the left side of the building. "Yes, we see you now. How long is the timer set for?" Another pause. "I see, good, we'll talk later."

As Jacob reached his car, everyone in the immediate area heard something in the distance, rapidly approaching. At first, Segel wasn't sure what the noise was. For a moment, he thought it might be an eighteen-wheeler or a train, but the highway was at least five miles away, and there were no train tracks nearby.

The noise changed, the pitch lowering, sounding more feral and animalistic. Segel was about to ask Macaria what it was when it grew louder, more intense, rapidly approaching. "What the…" Segel began to speak when the stranger overtook a passing car, crossed over the sidewalk, and headed straight for the government building. In that moment, Segel realized he was in real trouble, like he had never faced before. "Oh my God, it's him," was all he could utter as his mind went blank.

TWENTY-ONE

Alex ran down Four Mile Rd faster than he ran the night before and the world became a massive blur. His lungs took in more oxygen than earlier, and the rich blood flowed faster throughout his body. His eagle vision scanned the side of the road for the government complex ahead of him, as he tried to quickly adjust to the more vibrant colors, and what could only be described as a panoramic view, because his peripheral vision now allowed Alex to see almost two-hundred and seventy degrees, plus Alex still found the bluish/ amethyst white, ultraviolet spectrum disorienting. It was almost like trying to take in a full fireworks show and only seeing certain pyrotechnics.

Since he was literally running down the middle of the road Alex was forced to scan both lanes of the black top, While keeping an eye open for any traffic Because the last thing he needed was to get hit by an oncoming vehicle, but he began to feel he could easily clear an eighteen-wheeler, lengthwise but wasn't going to tempt fate if the chance presented itself.

As he overtook a blue Mini Cooper by a gas station, Alex

knew he must be getting close to the complex. Even though he was looking ahead on the road, his peripheral vision was wide enough to tell him the government building was coming up on his left, fast. Once he passed a couple of houses on the same side of the road as the gas station and the complex he crossed the road at the parking lot entrance, just avoiding an oncoming motorcycle. With his speed, sight, and enhanced reflexes Alex was positive he could avoid the Japanese crotch rocket.

Alex practically flew over the sidewalk, leaping almost twenty feet easily, landing on a patch of grass lining an area between the road and the complex, as he scanned for the huge black man he saw plant the bomb in his vision.

He stood there for a minute in the middle of the parking lot, scanning the area for his prey. "Where are you," he whispered out loud to himself then he saw Jacob at the end of the parking lot. And once Alex saw him his animal instincts took over. With his fists clenched in anger, Alex could feel eyes on him. His vision and hearing picked up the fear and concern in the faces and voices, but he didn't care—there was no time.

In seven seconds, Alex ran six steps, then leapt nearly thirty feet over the parking lot, landing next to Jacob, who'd just reached his car, surprising the enforcer with his entrance. "What the hell..." Jacob growled but stopped when Alex shoved Jacob into the side of his car, pinning the much larger man against the blue convertible, who despite his formidable size was at first shocked, then alarmed when he realized he couldn't push Alex off him.

Jacob loudly yelled, "What the hell's with you? Get away from me!"

"I'm going to ask one time, where is it?" Alex demanded. "The bomb?"

"What bomb? I don't have any idea what you're talking

about," Jacob denied Alex's accusations while continuing to struggle against the smaller man.

Alex saw the confusion in Jacob's eyes and knew the man was trying to understand how he had been caught and why he couldn't break free. Alex's strength was undeniable. He realized Jacob had no idea just how much stronger Alex was, despite his struggling efforts to push Alex away. Finally, Alex noticed Jacob's gaze fixated on his face, perceiving two things: first, how his eyes seemed wider and more angular, almost like a bird's eyes; and second, the intensity of Alex's predatory stare. Alex finally Jacob realized he was facing something entirely unfamiliar, and he recognized a chill of fear run through Jacob's body.

Alex gave a final shove to pin Jacob against his car, then clutched Jacob's thick neck with his left hand. "The bomb, tell me or I'll make sure you're at ground zero when it explodes, you bastard!" Alex realized they had attracted a crowd and he had to get the people out of the area. "Call the police and run," he yelled as loud as he could. "There's a bomb in the building somewhere!"

Alex heard the people as if they were using bullhorns and there was a lot of disbelief and discussion going on.

Jacob kept protesting as he struggled. "Get this psycho off of me!" At nearly six foot ten and three hundred and sixty pounds, the enforcer was not used to begging for help.

Jacob shook his head, scared, but refused to answer.

Jacob reached around to his back with his right hand and pulled a chrome-plated handgun from his rear belt holster. Jacob whipped the gun around, but as fast as he moved, he might as well have been standing still.

Alex saw the chrome automatic coming, released Jacob's throat, grabbing his right wrist instead. With his superior strength, Alex squeezed Jacob's wrist, crushing it and shattering all the bones around the joint.

"Ahhhh," Jacob screamed as he squeezed off a single round. Despite the echoing racket, Alex heard every bone crack and shatter.

Alex quickly realized that when the gunshot went off, most of the people in the parking lot ran for cover, screamed, or did both. Some panicked and ran from the government building. Alex didn't want anyone to get caught in a stampede and get hurt, but it did get people to move away from the site.

"Wrong choice. I meant what I said, you bastard. Tell me where the bomb is, or you get a front-row seat to Hiroshima." Alex knew he had to push Jacob over the edge. Pulling him away from the car, Alex heard Jacob's heart rate speed up. He grabbed Jacob by the chest and crotch, then, like a pro wrestler, gorilla pressed him over his head while letting out a growl that sounded like Shunkaha Wakinyan. To get Jacob to give up the location, Alex did the only thing he could think of. He took five steps from the blacktop onto the sidewalk in front of the government building, then dropped the larger man onto his shoulder and finally power slammed him onto the grass under several trees in front of the building.

Alex clenched his fists hard enough to make a cracking noise with his knuckles, stood over Jacob, who rolled onto his side, groaning like a wounded animal.

Alex recognized the fear in Jacob's face, it told the whole story. "Talk, or I'll plant you on the roof and you'll get the best seat in the house for the show."

Jacob gestured over his shoulder with his left thumb since he could barely move his right hand at this point. "It's on the gas meter, behind the building, near the air conditioners, now get me out of here!"

"If this building goes, you're going with it," Alex said,

knowing the first thing he had to do was evacuate the building.

Alex knew Jacob wasn't going anywhere, or at least anywhere fast, so he bolted into the glass vestibule, quickly scanned the walls, first in the vestibule then passed them into the reception area, where he found a wall mounted fire alarm, then rushed through the inner doors and pulled the switch. And immediately regretted his decision.

The whooping alarm and white strobe lights went off simultaneously, alerting everyone in the building to evacuate. Alex's senses were overwhelmed beyond description, leaving him nearly deaf and blind. As employees and visitors ran out into the parking lot, security rushed to the scene, and an officer demanded to know what was happening. But Alex couldn't respond; he was trying, unsuccessfully, to block out the lights and sounds. Despite his tightly shut eyes, the pulsating white light still flashed through, and the whooping alarm penetrated his hands covering his ears. It was completely pointless to try to protect himself, and for a few heart-stopping moments, Alex was completely paralyzed.

Dealing with the crippling sensory overload, Alex's head and heart urged him to move, but he couldn't. With alarms blaring, people rushing past him, and a guard trying to question him, something happened in Alex's mind. An image appeared in his mind's eye. At first, it was fuzzy, but it quickly cleared once he focused on a vision of Grandmother. She had only one thing to say: "Alexander, move!"

Unexpectedly Alex blocked out the world around him. His mind reached a different place, and nothing could touch it now. Alex rushed past security and the workers running from the complex. Once outside, Alex ran with all his strength. As he turned the corner of the building, his peripheral vision caught Jacob pulling himself up, trying to head towards his car, but by the way he was moving Alex knew he hurt him. *No way you're escaping you bastard,* Alex thought. He ran full out, aiming for Jacob, then shoulder-blocked him as if Jacob were a blocking sled. The impact was so powerful that the massive man flew into the side of one of the elm trees landscaping the complex.

Alex turned the corner, and kept running towards the rear of the building, praying that Jacob hadn't lied. His vision showed him a bomb, but not the exact location, which had him silently swearing. In less than ten seconds Alex was at the rear of the building, where he saw more people rushing away, out the back doors, and into the rear parking lot, further towards safety.

Alex accelerated around a bulging portion of the build-ing, passing by a rear security door. Right ahead of him loomed the massive A.C. unit, and Alex finally saw the gas meter and the bomb zip-tied to it. When Alex reached the bomb, it occurred to him that he didn't know what to do.

Something told Alex there wasn't enough time to wait for the Marshals or the Bomb Squad. He heard an electronic beep going off every second, indicating the countdown. Alex figured it had been about five minutes since he first saw Jacob planting the bomb in his vision. He could finally hear emergency vehicles rushing toward the complex, but his wolf's hearing told him they'd be too late. The beeping had sped up and was going faster. With a sense of urgency, Alex knew he had to act quickly.

Taking a deep breath to steady himself, Alex carefully placed his left hand on top of the bomb to keep it stable. Using his right hand, he wedged his first and middle fingers between the pipe from the gas meter and the zip-tie. It was a tight fit, but with some delicate maneuvering of the casing, Alex managed to insert his fingers. The next part was tricky —he needed to open his fingers like a pair of scissors.

Normally, breaking the zip-tie, this way would be impossible, but with the strength of a bear, the plastic snapped. Alex immediately grabbed the bomb with both hands to prevent it from falling.

The beeping was steady, which Alex assumed was a good thing. Then he thought, *What do I do with the damned thing?*

Alex looked around for options. He saw people, the occupied buildings, the nearby library, and the gas station further down 4 Mile Road. His eyes landed on an empty field across the road from the government building. He considered it for a moment, but something told him to forget it. It was almost two hundred yards away, with employees and visitors standing on the sidewalk directly across from the field after evacuating the building.

As Alex scanned the grounds, searching for an option, he found one. A dumpster was close by, and he went for it. Cupping the bomb like a football, he prayed it wouldn't detonate with all the movement. Gingerly, he carried the device to the dumpster, lifted the lid, and tried to ignore the stench from the reeking garbage inside. He placed the bomb inside, surrounded by several trash bags. Then realized the dumpster was on wheels, and Alex knew he could get it further away from the buildings. After quickly unlocking the wheels, he got behind the dark blue container and pushed. Normally, he wouldn't have been able to do this, but with the speed of a mountain lion and the strength of a bear, he easily moved the load towards the empty field behind the government building, away from the gas meter. "Nothing to it, but to do it," he told himself.

As Alex pushed the dumpster further away from the buildings, it finally and completely occurred to him. Any doubts he had in his parents' living room, dealing with the Trax, and when he was with Wolfhart and Grandmother, were completely gone. Using the gifts from his animal allies, Alex fully believed this was all true and was now embracing his destiny.

When far enough away, he gave a final shove towards the field, then ran like hell back the way he'd come. Alex braced himself for the eruption and prayed that no one would be hurt.

A couple people in the parking lot, who'd seen Alex before were trying to ask him questions like, "Who are you?", "What's this about?", and "What's going on?" when they got a very frank answer.

When the bomb exploded, Alex could only look away and grit his teeth. The explosion erupted with a deafening roar that seemed to rip the air apart. It reverberated through the ground and echoed off the buildings, followed by a sharp crackle as debris was hurled in all directions. The shockwave created a tangible force, a pressure that hit like a physical blow, leaving a ringing in the ears of anyone nearby, particularly Alex.

The explosion propelled a sizeable fireball skyward, which only destroyed the dumpster and a small patch of the field, but the first explosion was quickly followed by a second blast, indicating the device was more powerful than initially believed.

Everyone who witnessed, heard, or felt the explosion was shell-shocked, except for Alex, who turned, then raced past the crowd. He still had Jacob to deal with.

Alex approached the front of the building while ignoring the chaos from the crowd and the approaching sirens from the emergency vehicles. He realized the sirens were coming from all directions. Most of the employees rushed towards the rear to see what happened as first responders arrived in force. Officers from the State Police Department, the Silver Creek Police Department, and volunteers from the Irving and Cattaraugus Reservation Fire Departments all converged on the scene.

The only two people who weren't looking at the blast site were Alex and Jacob. The latter was trying to pull himself up to his feet with a young tree, dragging himself after being bodychecked, while the former stalked him like a predator hunting its prey.

"Going somewhere?" Alex asked, just before clenching his right fist again, cracking his knuckles. Jacob turned and with a defeated look on his face, he just shook his melon sized head. "Good, cause I know a lot of folks are going to want to talk to us both."

TWENTY-TWO

Even though he watched the explosion like everyone else, Segel was also looking out for the stranger. He realized things were going sideways when Jacob was turned into a human medicine ball and Segel knew his plans were falling apart. From the backseat he said, "Get me out of here, now."

Like her employer, Macaria was stunned in silence. She sat there watching, impressed with what she saw. The stranger reminded her of Lonestar, a member of Texas' team of heroes, the Border Patrol. She was intrigued and wanted to get to know all about this man.

"Not in five minutes, I mean now," Segel emphasized by slapping the top of Macaria seat, which woke her up.

"Uh right," she said then started the engine. "Where to, the office?" Macaria asked as the BMW began creeping from the parking lot, waiting for traffic to pass.

"No, home," Segel resentfully grunted out under his breath, knowing he'd have to form a new plan, fast.

The sirens finally died down, and first responders rushed towards the building as Alex walked back towards the front of the property, literally dragging Jacob in hand. He gave him one warning, "Try anything stupid and you'll become the world's largest lawn dart." Alex had the larger man's right arm in a chicken wing, with his right hand nearly between his shoulder blades.

Jacob asked, "You gotta do this? It's humiliating."

"It's this or I carry you like a sack of kitty litter over my shoulder. I guess I could trust you to behave yourself," Alex shot back sarcastically "I think you know by now you're out of your weight class, now behave yourself, you bastard."

"I'll walk," Jacob replied, then said, "You know I'm going to sue you." Jacob was favoring his left side, tending to his ribs, where Alex had plowed into him. "Besides, you got no legal right to detain me."

"Consider this a citizen's arrest, and as for being sued I'll take my chances. Move!"

Alex knew it was time to explain everything or at least try to. He looked for a sheriff or another officer. He forced Jacob towards the vestibule doors, attempting to get the attention of the first responders. "There's no fire," Alex shouted, then realized some of the people there were witnesses who watched him in the parking lot, and pointed him out to the officials, as if the site of him manhandling the much larger black man wasn't enough to draw attention.

They told the authorities about the explosion and how Alex placed the bomb into the dumpster then shoved it into the empty field.

As Alex stopped, he held Jacob, tight and gave one warning, "Run or try anything stupid and I'll break the bones in all four of your limbs for an opener, after that I get nasty." Jacob just nodded slightly, knowing he couldn't win this fight.

"What do you mean there's no fire?" one of the responders yelled.

"This man planted a bomb, and the building had to be cleared as fast as possible," Alex explained. That's when the questions came in from all sides and for a moment Alex's hearing was overloaded and it was too much.

Alex finally saw the man who was charge approach him. His gold badge read Cattaraugus Reservation Marshal, and the name tag had the name Hill, both pinned to his tan and brown uniform shirt. Alex guessed Hill was about fifteen years younger than Wolfhart, but he also had a weathered face and dark, grey hair.

Hill made his presence be known immediately by announcing to his deputies, "I want this site secured! Back this crowd away from the building, over by the library." Hill's men and the other first responders moved with a purpose.

Hill and three of his deputies turned their attention to Alex and Jacob. The look on Hill's experienced face spoke volumes, surprise. "Who the hell are you and what is going on?" Hill demanded, as his deputies began moving people across the way and the first responders double-checked the site for any more explosives.

Alex realized there was a hint of recognition in his expression, but as far as he knew he never met the man. He also knew this was going to be a problem, so he figured it best to play it straight, "My name's Alex Harlow, this man placed a bomb on the gas main in the back of the building Marshall Hill. I put it into a dumpster then pushed it into the empty field so no one would get hurt. I admit to pulling the fire alarm to clear the building, because I didn't know if I could get the bomb away in time."

Hill listened and at first was silent, standing with a semi-slack jawed look, then tore into Alex. "I hope you've got a good lawyer, cause you're gonna need one for every law you broke," sounding like he was coming right out of a cliched 1970's movie or television show.

"That won't be necessary Hill," suddenly Wolfhart seemingly appeared out of nowhere.

Hill just shook his head with a semi-smile, then just said "Oh Shit. Look at what the cat puked up." Hill then went on after bracing himself. "All right bonehead, what in the hell are you doing here, this is a secured site."

Alex wondered the same thing. The looks on their faces told Alex there was history between them, but it didn't look like there were any fond memories.

Hill approached Wolfhart clenching his fist. "I heard you died. Man, I hate it when good news turns out to be a load of horseshit."

Wolfhart returned fire. "Sorry to disappoint you, but I want to be sure I'm around to piss on your grave. Tell me, are you still beating confessions out of speeders or just still taking bribes you bastard."

As they got within a foot of each other the tension rose, and Alex thought he was going to have to help the deputies separate them.

Then without warning the mood changed like a fast-flowing current. Wolfhart laughed and stuck out his hand. "Damn good to see you, Johnny."

They shook hands and Hill, who began laughing too, said, "Still ugly as ever. Glad to see you too, Nicky-boy. You're looking good brother, but what do you have to do with them," Hill asked, thumbing at Alex and Jacob with his weathered right hand.

"Alex, let me introduce Johnny 'Hawk' Hill, head of the Reservation's Marshall Service, and one of my best friends. Johnny, this is Alex Harlow, my grandson."

The disbelief on Hill's face came back and, once the realization hit him, Hill asked, "Ojistah's son?"

Wolfhart gave half a nod.

Under his breath Hill let a slight "Wow," out. "Well, it's nice to meet ya, but I gotta know what the hell's going on?"

"Simple, this jackoff," Alex began, gesturing with his head towards Jacob, who Alex was still holding onto, "attempted to blow the building up and he's going to tell us everything."

Hill looked to Wolfhart, then back to Alex and Jacob, surprised that the massive, black man hadn't resisted or tried to escape. "Why's he gonna do that?"

"Because, Marshall," Alex said, while giving a predatory smile at Jacob, then clenched his fists hard enough to crack his knuckles, "I'm going to ask him nicely." Satisfied when Alex saw the uneasy look on Jacob's face, he added, "And because if he doesn't tell us everything, it'll be time to stop being nice."

"Easy, I'll talk," Jacob said. "I'll speak to you all, the reservation leaders and the Feds, but in return for certain considerations. I'll turn over my employer and his plans, as far as I know them." He then turned towards Alex. "But I need a doctor, and I don't mind being cuffed—it's not my first time. Just get me away from this maniac!"

Alex smiled, looked at Hill, who took out his steel handcuffs from his black, duty belt.

———

In less than ten minutes, Alex and Wolfhart—who was allowed to tag along since he could answer Hill's questions more easily than Alex could—found themselves with Hill, Jacob (who was secured by a deputy), and Cattaraugus President C. Gary Highbanks. The group stood in the vestibule after the first responders finished clearing the building. After a hasty introduction and a complex explanation, Hill questioned Jacob about the bombing and Segel's intent.

Everyone surrounded Jacob during the questioning, except for Alex and Wolfhart, who were off to the side talking privately. "Okay how'd you get here so fast, speed of the mountain lion?"

Smirking Wolfhart shook his head and answered, "Grandmother and the Sanctuary, it sends you where you need to be, which is how you wound up out here so fast. 'Sides, I thought it best to smooth things over with Hill and the others. This whole thing was going to take a lot of explaining and I've got answers you can't provide, yet."

Alex admitted to himself Wolfhart was right about that, and a lot more.

They got quiet when Hill came over and informed them what Jacob gave up. "All right, his boss, Segel is a billionaire industrialist, who wants the land. Turns out we're sitting on top of some material Segel thinks he can put to use. The original plan was to pay for everyone to move and somehow get the government to approve, given that this is a reservation. Highbanks confirmed that part, cause he had a meeting with Segel earlier. If the deal went through Segel would dig up the material and do whatever he wanted with it.

"Also, the big guy confessed to killing some poor schlub, named Beck. Worked for the D.E.C. He followed Segel's orders to dump Beck into the Niagara River. I heard a body was found up there the other day, but there was no I.D. on him, so identifying him may take time." Hill then looked right at Alex, "Apparently, he's more afraid of you than his boss. You must be something kid."

"You've no idea, sir, I can barely believe it myself."

"Why the bomb?" Wolfhart asked while looking over Jacob with contempt in his eyes.

"Yeah, Highbanks and his boys turned Segel down flat. The bomb was Segel's way of clearing the decks for any opposition from future leaders he might approach. Turns out the man has a problem with taking no for an answer."

"Any idea where Segel is now," Wolfhart asked as Alex stared at Jacob through a glass partition, listening to every word, while Jacob stared right back at him.

"Not quite," Hill admitted while looking over his shoulder at Jacob, then looked back at Alex, shaking his head. "He says Segel could be either at his office in Getzville or at his place in Harris Hill. I've already made calls for warrants, but..."

"By the time the paperwork goes through Segel will be out of the area easy," Wolfhart cut in with. "Maybe to somewhere he can't be extradited from, right?"

"Right," Hill said as he pulled out a worn, brown leather cigar case that held three cigars on the inside and a tarnished cutter clipped onto the outside. As he pulled one out and measured it for a trimming, Hill added, "I'd give a year's pay to get him now."

Alex, who had been silent, went into a trance-like state. His head rose upwards, his mouth went slack, then his eyes took on an avian appearance.

Hill was about to ask what was happening when Wolfhart raised his left hand, signaling him to stay quiet. Seeing Alex like this, Wolfhart knew what was happening and asked his grandson, "Alex, what do you see?"

"A black car, pulling into a estate, north of here. Two people, a man and a woman, running into a Tudor style mansion."

Hill asked Wolfhart, "Is he for real?"

"You trusted Wildrun when you were a deputy, didn't

you?" Finally, Wolfhart opened up to his longtime friend, "I know it's a leap of faith, Johnny," then he gave Hill a truer sense of the picture, "Trust Alex as much as you'd trust the Red Warrior or Wildrun."

"Yeah, but this, this is…" Hill was literally speechless as he began to understand the whole picture.

Then Wolfhart asked Alex, "Can you stop them?"

"If I go now, yes, I will stop Segel." There was something different in Alex's voice, a boldness that hadn't been there before. It wasn't arrogance, but a new confidence that declared Alex knew what he was capable of, and he'd finish what he set out to do.

Wolfhart realized his grandson was not the same man he was twenty-four hours ago. "Well?" Wolfhart asked Hill.

"I don't know, Nick," Hill said, his hand beginning to unconsciously shake. "I get what you're saying, but this has gotta be legal."

"Johnny, you remember the Isolationists Statute? You can make it official. Alex can legally detain Segel, as a represen-tative of the reservation, if he catches him. At least he can stop the bastard from running until the state police or the feds show up. I've heard about Segel. He's got half the money in the world at his disposal. Don't you think he'll try to get away as soon as possible?"

After a moment of consideration, Hill nodded. "Yeah, you're right. Enough has been taken from us." Hill listened intently, pondered for a moment, and then, with one of his cheap cigars held between his left fingers, quickly nodded in agreement.

Alex asked, "What's this statute you're talking about?"

Hill quickly explained. "Back in the thirties, the Isola-tionists were a team of heroes from the Big Apple. The District Attorney managed to get a law passed that allowed folks like you to testify in court without revealing their secret identities. Eventually, the law was amended to allow metahumans to be deputized and grant them arrest powers, but it's no different than any other officer."

Alex recalled reading about the Isolationists, a team of fervent non-interventionist heroes who supported the "America First" movement. They believed the country should focus on its own defense and avoid entangling alliances—until December of 1941 that is.

Hill glanced at Wolfhart and added, "There've been a few times we've needed to execute the law here on the Res." He then marched right up to Alex, pointed at his broad chest, and accusingly asked, "How positive are you that you can find him?"

A grim look overtook Alex's face. "Say the word and he's yours, Marshall."

Hill smiled, then said "We'll make it official later, son. Get that sonuvabitch."

Alex nodded, turned, then walked through the glass doors, and got into Jacob's face and demanded one thing. "Where does your boss live?"

Feeling disheartened by his defeat and fully aware of what was coming, Jacob let out a long, deflating sigh and finally gave in. "Harris Hill, across from the country club, 8885 Greiner, it's a huge Tudor mansion, with wrought iron fencing lining the property."

Without another word, Alex started for the parking lot entrance. Meanwhile, Jacob glared at him, his eyes promising that their time for reckoning would come.

———

Outside the building, Alex heard Wolfhart running, trying to keep up with him. "Alex, go back to the Sanctuary first!

Grandmother will make sure you get to where you're needed!"

Hill followed a step behind Wolfhart, then called out for Alex to hold up a moment. "Ted, get over here," Hill yelled when he saw one of his deputies. The twenty-something-year-old ran over from his crowd control duty.

"Alex, before you go, you'll need this," Hill said, turning to the hesitant kid who looked like a high school freshman. "Ted, this man needs to borrow your badge." Hill saw the questions forming on his deputy's face and answered his concerns. "You're not in trouble, but I need to deputize this man right now."

Without question, Ted followed orders, unpinned his badge, and handed it over. "Alex, hold up your right hand," Hill instructed. Alex did as told, giving Wolfhart a confused look. "I don't remember the exact words, but say, 'I swear.'" Alex complied.

"Is this necessary?" Alex asked.

"Yeah, this has gotta be legal," Hill said. "I hereby deputize Alexander Harlow as a member of the Cattaraugus Indian Reservation Deputy Sheriff's Office and authorize him with all the powers and responsibilities of this position." Hill then handed the badge to Alex, who immediately pinned it on his shirt. "Under The Isolationists' statute, Alexander Harlow is now a special officer for the sheriff's office and is authorized to hold for questioning Regino Segel and any associates involved with the attempted bombing of the Cattaraugus Indian Reservation Government Building."

Hill finally took the cigar that had been between his fingers all this time, cut the end off, put it in his mouth, and lit it up. After one good puff, he said, "Okay, Deputy Harlow, do your duty."

After giving a half nod to Hill, Alex dashed back toward the Sanctuary with a burst of speed, moving with the agility of a mountain lion, leaving everyone astonished at his swiftness.

Hill stood there with Wolfhart, shaking his head in disbelief, amazed at Alex's speed. He finally lit his cigar and then offered one to Wolfhart, who took it, bit off the end, spat it out, and lit it.

"I don't believe it's happening all over again, Nick," Hill said between two long puffs.

Wolfhart stared in the direction Alex had run. He corrected him, "No, Johnny, this is all new." Then he looked the law enforcement officer in the eye and said, "This isn't like before. Alex is the Rainbow Warrior."

TWENTY-THREE

Segel finished a phone call as Macaria pulled into the driveway of the estate. "Have the jet fueled and ready to take off once I arrive. How long will it take to reach Podgorica?" After a brief pause Segel said, "Just over nine hours, all right. We'll be at the airport in less than an hour." He hung up.

"Where are we going?" Macaria asked.

"Podgorica, the capital city of Montenegro, in Europe. It's close to the Adriatic and most importantly Montenegro doesn't have an extradition treaty with the United States," Segel said as he got out of the car.

He rushed through the front door, with Macaria close on his heels. "I think it's best to move operations overseas and let the lawyers handle things for the time being. We can work from Europe for years."

Macaria never saw him like this before. "So, we're running." It was more a statement than a question.

Segel felt unnerved and maybe was truly feeling fear for the first time in his life. He snapped back, staring into her dark eyes. "Think of it as a strategic withdrawal. Go upstairs, get your passport, and pack what you need. I want to be at the airstrip in thirty minutes."

Without another word, he rushed across the grand foyer, his footsteps echoing off the black-and-white marble tiles and rich dark wood-paneled walls, which gleamed under the chandelier's soft light. Segel ignored the large, ornate mirrors he usually paused before each day to check for any imperfections and headed past the antique polished mahogany console table towards his study as Macaria moved up the dark wood, grand staircase that spiraled up to the second floor, like a shadow to her bedroom.

Segel charged into his study like a stampeding herd of bison, heading straight for the bottom drawer of his desk. He pulled out a strongbox, unlocked it, and retrieved a newly developed weapon from S.I.'s weapons division. It looked like the lovechild of an automatic and a shock baton —jet black and chrome, yet compact, smaller than a standard .38.

Segel took off his topcoat and suit jacket, rolled up his right shirt sleeve, and plugged in the weapon's battery, a power source about the size of an MP3. Finally, he pulled out a black wrist sleeve attached to a small, movable rail, fastening the weapon to it at the front. With everything securely in place, Segel was ready, his arm poised for action.

Once ready, Segel approached the portrait of Napoleon Crossing the Alps. He pulled it away from the wall, revealing a safe embedded in the dark oak. He spun the dial and retrieved important documents, his passport, ten stacks of bank-wrapped cash totaling one million dollars, and a small metal travel box. With relief, he confirmed the box still held diamonds, emeralds, sapphires, pearls, and opals on the top level, and twelve small stacks of gold coins on the bottom. He quickly packed everything into a small briefcase, snapped it shut, and locked it.

Stepping out of the office Segel yelled, "Ready?"

A moment later Macaria came rushing down, carrying her Go Bag, to which she added a few more items, since this was unexpected. Retreating wasn't in the woman's nature, and she hated the idea. "Yes, fortunately I'm usually prepared for making swift travel preparations."

Knowing they could obtain whatever they needed once out of the country, Segel felt a sense of relief. He could always send for certain items if necessary. Most importantly, leaving would give him the one thing he needed more than anything else right now: time.

Once airborne, with Western New York behind him, Segel would feel better and already planned a "I was called out of the country on emergency business" story, but he knew Jacob might be problematic.

Once back in the car, they were ready to rush to a private airstrip adjacent to the Buffalo International Airport in Cheektowaga, NY.

As Macaria reversed down the driveway she asked, "Do you have a place set up for us yet?"

Logging onto his tablet Segel said no. "Once we're airborne, I'll contact the office manager in Getzville and inform him that I've been called out of town on business. I'll also make hotel reservations for us. After we arrive, I'll speak with a real estate agent."

"Then what?" asked the native from Lubbock, Texas, her eyes darting between the side mirrors and the rearview mirror above her.

"Jacob can say whatever he wants to the authorities, but it'll be their job to prove his accusations. However, if it comes to it, I'll have him taken care of."

It wouldn't be the first time he had someone murdered, but Jacob would be the first in Segel's inner circle marked for death. Segel already had someone in mind. Since they were in the Buffalo area, the professional only known as Holy Cross could be an option, if available.

As they reached the foot of the driveway, Macaria asked, "Any idea what you're gonna tell your uncle?" Suddenly, a violent jolt stopped the BMW, and the impact stampeded through their bodies. Both believed Macaria had collided with a passing car or truck.

"What the hell did you hit?" Segel yelled at Macaria, as he righted himself.

As Macaria steadied herself, she was about to tell Segel she hadn't hit anything when she saw the truth in the rear-view mirror. She couldn't speak.

"What's with you?" Segel demanded as he picked up his tablet and case from the car floor. As he pulled himself up, he said, "Didn't you hear me? What did…" His voice trailed off as he looked in the rearview mirror and saw a figure. At first, he thought they had hit a pedestrian. The truth dawned on him, and Segel realized he was now in real trouble.

Alex stood there, holding back the car, and the look on his face spoke volumes.

———

At first, Alex just held the car in place, but then he started pushing on the trunk with all his strength. The muscles in his hands strained, and the veins on the tops of his hands bulged visibly. He gritted his teeth as his calf and thigh muscles strained, but he stood firm.

Segel and Macaria looked back at Alex in stunned disbelief. "What are you waiting for," Segel ordered, without saying the actual words.

"Hang on," she yelled back.

Suddenly, Alex felt the car push back hard as Macaria

gripped the wheel and floored the gas pedal. For a minute, it was a stalemate: the luxury car against a metahuman possessed with the strength of a grizzly. The rear tires locked up, while the front ones spun and smoked, the engine roaring. Soon, the driveway resembled a burnout pit at a racetrack. The noise and odor began to get to Alex, but he didn't relent. He had given his word. Segel watched as Alex gripped the trunk, dug his heels into the ground, and pushed back, hard.

Finally, with uncharacteristic panic in his voice, Segel yelled, "Do something!"

Macaria, with a slight smile on her face, replied, "All right, watch this." She shifted gears, and they jolted forward, fast.

"What are you doing?" Segel demanded.

"Doing something," Macaria yelled back, as they rapidly approached the closed door of the attached four-car garage, she quickly shifted gears again, throwing the car into reverse and accelerating, aiming for Alex.

"Whoever he is, he's about to be roadkill," Macaria boasted. "Damn shame, he's cute," she added, glancing at the display screen on the dashboard that showed the rear camera's image. Despite the onboard computer's warning, she kept going.

As the car hurtled towards him, Alex, either out of natural fear, pure survival instinct, or perhaps something more, threw his right hand up with all five fingers extended. Suddenly, the driveway erupted.

The ground rose up like a rapidly growing tree, forming a curved ramp in mere seconds. When the car hit the solid mass of rock and dirt, it went up in reverse, following the curve of the incline. The luxury automobile raced up, sped to Alex's right, and finally crashed hard on its passenger side. The impact severely jarred both Segel and Macaria, while leaving a metallic, echoing thud in Alex's ears.

Once the car stopped rocking, Alex marched over and used his strength to push it upright. Two of its wheels were flattened from the impact, and the entire passenger side looked as if it had been sideswiped by an eighteen-wheeler, with the panels and doors resembling wrinkled black tin foil. The side windows were spider-webbed, and Alex could smell the odor of oil and gas leaking from the passenger side.

Walking around to the driver's side, Alex stood with clenched fists, waiting for Segel and Macaria to regain their composure. Segel, normally calm and cold, looked shell-shocked, like a man who had survived a natural disaster.

Macaria took longer to steady herself. Her eyes shut and hands on her temples, she attempted to catch her breath. "What the hell was that?" she quietly asked.

Segel could only say, "It's him," while shaking his head.

Still trying to compose herself, Macaria asked, "Him? Who's him?" Her answer came in a way she never expected.

Alex grabbed the rear driver's side door and ripped it off its hinges. The noise was comparable to a wounded, dying animal. "Regino Segel, you're wanted for questioning in the attempted bombing of the Cattaraugus Indian Reservation government building and for attempting to run me over!"

Alex saw Segel didn't know what to say or do in that moment, or he assumed he was stalling for time.

When Segal finally spoke, he went on the offensive. He slid out of the backseat, giving a once over at the damage as he came out. Alex decided the criminal was either impressed or stunned. "Who the hell are you, and what makes you think you can damage my property?"

"When your driver tried to turn me into a speed bump it became self-defense," Alex snapped back.

"You tried to stop us from leaving. You didn't answer my question." That's when Macaria pulled herself from the driver's seat.

"I did more than try," Alex said with a hint of cockiness. "Like I said you're wanted for questioning in attempted bombing of the Cattaraugus Reservation Government Building."

Alex saw him adopt his polished, professional facade he likely used when dealing with officials, competitors, or anyone he wanted something from. "Oh my, that sounds serious," then noticed the badge pinned to Alex's chest. Segel looked at Macaria. Alex glimpsed the woman whom, he decided, seemed to be quickly evaluating the situation and calculating a plan, fast.

Segel said, "Tell me something, on whose authority are you stopping me and my driver? What law enforcement agency do you work for? Granted, I haven't heard any agencies in this country employing metahumans."

"I've been authorized to detain you until the Reservation Marshals, local and state authorities arrive to question you. The Isolationists' Statute from the 1930s allows me to aid law enforcement and arrest you, if need be. I already have you and your driver for assault on a special officer," Alex said, dialing back his intensity to make it easier for Segel to comply. "You have the right to remain silent," and like that Alex recited the Miranda Warning.

———

Alex's tone told Macaria he was serious, and the situation was escalating fast. She didn't know where things were headed, but she prepped herself by reaching under her long, dark gray topcoat and unsnapping her holster belt. Wanting to see how Segel would play it, she didn't go any further. She was surprised when Segel began to smile and nod.

"It is you, isn't it?" Segel said, pointing a still shaky finger at Alex. "You're the one who stopped those punks behind the arena last night, didn't you?" Alex remained silent, but his quietness confirmed Segel's suspicion. "Don't deny it," Segel said, his grin widening. "Speed, strength, Geokinesis of some type, enhanced vision—I'm betting by the look of your eyes—and God only knows what else you're capable of."

Macaria saw how Alex kept an eye on both of them. Even though he was mainly looking at Segel as they talked, she noticed how Alex's "eagle eyes" noticed every move either of them made, along with passing traffic and a couple walking their dog a block away. She saw how focused Alex was on the job at hand.

"My friend," Segel said, putting on his best salesman and P.T. Barnum façade, "I could use a man like you on my payroll. If you know who I am, then you must know my company is a worldwide major player in several industries and ventures. Someone of your talents would be an asset of amazing proportions." Then Segel brought out the big guns. "I've got one million dollars in cash in that case, in the car," he said, pointing to the interior. "Let's call it a signing bonus, plus a regular salary we can discuss, but with seven zeros at the end."

"Let me guess the rest," Alex interrupted, "Money and more, let's say perks down the road for what, helping you two reach a private jet and get away?"

Macaria saw Segel smile, giving a half nod, expecting Alex to take the bait and swallow, since he believed everyone had a price.

Alex stood his ground and proudly upset Segel. "No deal. First, I'm not for sale. Second, I gave my word to the

Marshal. Third, you are going to pay for your crimes," Alex declared. "Easy or hard, it's your choice Segel, but you're going one way or the other."

Furious rage filtered across Segel's face, but Macaria saw it, even if he tried hiding it. No more fear and panic could be seen on his face any longer. He was furious. Macaria knew her boss couldn't buy off this 'hero', because men like him had honor and integrity, much like his father, which was another reason she knew Segel hated Alex. Macaria caught Segel's eye, and he gave her a secret hand signal, which she'd been expecting.

"I could offer you a lot more, mister," Segel said, "but I have a feeling your answer would be the same, right?"

Alex nodded slowly, not taking his eyes off Segel.

"So that leaves me one more option," Segel said. As the words left his mouth, Macaria moved like a jaguar stalking its prey, then swiftly and stealthily struck.

She pulled her modified Glock 34 from her right hip, thumbed the hammer back, and aimed it almost point-blank at Alex's skull. Macaria moved with ice-cold precision, but her speed and skills were no match for Alex's reflexes.

Alex caught sight of the gun as soon as she flinched, leaving a UV trail in mid-air. Instinctively, he raised his left hand, and suddenly a gust of wind arose from nowhere. The intensity was akin to that of a tornado in the Midwest, completely focused on Macaria. The windshear took everyone by surprise, including Alex.

Macaria's gun flew across the driveway, landing on the other side of the lawn, as she struggled to stay upright and on her feet. With everyone's attention on Macaria, Segel made the mistake of twisting his forearm and wrist, unspringing his handgun, and taking direct aim at Alex.

Once it came out, Alex grabbed Segel's wrist, squeezing harder than most humans ever could. "AHHHHHH," Segel screamed as crushing pain shot through his hand and wrist. "OH MY GOD, STOP," he yelled, begging for the first time in his life, with actual tears forming.

Seeing Segel in trouble, Macaria acted swiftly. She pulled her hidden belly knife from her belt and lunged at Alex, but he easily anticipated her move.

Alex immediately lifted Segel by his wrist, then turned and slapped Macaria down, rag dolling him into her. They both flew at least ten feet, tumbling onto and past the drive-way. The knife was lost somewhere in the bushes and trees lining the property

Standing over them, Alex said, "Right now, you're down to two options: one, surrender and wait for the authorities, then take your punishment like a man. Two, resist, and I promise you it goes from bad to worse, faster and harder than you can ever imagine." Alex watched as they pulled themselves up, unsteadily at first, not believing the situation.

Macaria was slowly beginning to accept that Alex was a metahuman who would stop them—there was no doubt in her mind. Segel was another matter.

———

Segel possessed a darkness in his soul, an abyss that had taken human form. All-consuming, filled with hate and rage that could never be satisfied, he was like a rabid animal that would eventually have to be put down. Segel was someone who could kill his parents and perform copious scores of immoral acts without hesitation, as if they were nothing. But suddenly, Alex noticed something in Segel snapped. Alex thought of his previous words and realized Segel was reacting to the use of the words "like a man" and seemed to trigger a deep-seated fury in him. Alex didn't know that these were the same words Segel's father used to push him growing up. Those three words had sent Segel into a blinding rage. He savagely yelled out loud at Alex, sounding more like a beast than a man. Extending his right arm and shouting, "DIE," before pulling the trigger.

In that moment, Alex realized two things: the weapon was attached to Segel's forearm, not just handheld, and it was no normal handgun. As soon as Alex realized this, Segel began to pull the trigger, and Alex moved fast. A reddish-golden energy beam materialized with an ear-piercing SKREECH, causing a small explosion that evaporated the ground where Alex had just been standing.

Alex had never seen anything like it before, and he didn't know what it did technically, but Alex was positive he didn't want to get hit by it, so he moved, only faster this time. He charged at Segel, who couldn't get a clear shot. Alex had already grabbed Segel's wrist, by the time the billionaire thought he had lined up a shot. Alex squeezed harder than before to control the man, who by now wasn't feeling any pain.

As they struggled, Alex pulled Segel closer, and despite Segel being almost half a foot taller, Alex drove his right elbow into Segel's face, shattering his nose. This allowed Alex to gain control, ripping the blaster, holster, and all away, tearing Segel's clothes in the process.

Finally, Alex lifted Segel by his topcoat and looked at the three-foot crater where he had been standing. The realization of what could have happened stunned him as the scent of charred earth penetrated his nostrils.

Alex felt an anger rise up in him like he never had before. He detected the unmistakable salty scent of blood in the air, which suddenly whet his mouth. Alex looked Segel in the eyes—saw the man's pain. "You bastard," was all Alex quietly said.

Despite the pain and fear he was feeling, the industrialist put on his businessman's face. "You know they'll never hold me. Oh, I might have a fine or some penalty to pay, but I'll never see the inside of a prison. That sort of thing doesn't apply to people like me. You know how many other businessmen, community leaders, and politicians never saw a day in prison."

Segel's out-of-control ego fully emerged, and hubris took over. "You should have taken my offer. I don't know who you are yet, but I will, and when I do, everyone you care about is dead. You won't know when or where, but you're going to need a football field to bury them all. And after your friends and family on the Res are dead, I will go to work on you. You're part of the world we live in, and I have access to people as powerful and dangerous—maybe more than you on both counts—and you won't be able to stop them all. All I have to do is sit back, wait, and watch." A sickening smile crept across Segel's face, then unexpectedly, he spat a bloodied shot into Alex's face.

Alex then let out a roar so loud that every animal within a five-mile radius took notice, recognizing a new alpha predator. In that moment, Alex was more animal than man, but a part of him, as a man, knew where to hurt Segel. He drove his fist as hard as he could into Segel's gut, and from the sounds he detected, Alex knew he had ruptured something in the man's body.

Just then a voice came to Alex's mind crying out with rage and fury, it screamed for blood, *"DESTROY HIM,"* it ordered Alex. *"HE TRIED TO KILL OUR BROTHERS AND SISTERS, HE THREATENED OUR LOVED ONES, HAS COMMITTED NUMEROUS CRIMES AGAINST MANKIND AND GRANDMOTHER EARTH! HE NEEDS TO BE PUT TO DEATH FOR THE GOOD OF ALL, FOR JUSTICE!"*

Alex stood there, unsure of what was happening. If it was a psychotic break, it would explain the past three days, or if the voice meant he had multiple personality disorder, which wasn't any better.

As Alex stood there, he finally realized he had Segel by the throat, with his hand around the man's windpipe, squeezing it, while Segel was finally on his knees. Alex wasn't sure when or how this happened, but he didn't like it, and for a moment he fought to regain control.

To the outside world, it was a moment, but internally it seemed to take much longer for Alex. He began to have another vision. He was back where he met Shunkaha Wakinyan, but now there was a different entity, one he'd never seen before—a female one. The upper half of her head looked like an owl's, with brown and white feathers and a beak, running down the left side of her face, as if she were wearing a mask. The remainder of her face was that of a beautiful woman. For a moment, Alex thought it was Marie in some kind of costume.

From the rear of her head extended a pair of deer antlers and ears. She was dressed in tan and brown buckskins, with fringed boots, and a pair of gray, brown, and white wings spread from her back. She looked at Alex—or rather, she looked through him—much like Shunkaha Wakinyan had. But Alex felt this was different. He began to feel calmer, more composed, peaceful, and balanced. The voice he had heard before was silenced, and he knew what to do.

Alex used a part of Segel's topcoat to wipe his face clean. "As much as I want to break you into a million pieces and see what else I'm capable of, I made a promise, and you are under arrest, you bastard."

As Segel attempted to regain his breath, he realized he might have internal damage, but his pride, ego, and vanity overrode his common sense. "I'm going to see you suffer in ways you can't imagine, you insignificant microbe. I don't know what you think you heard, but I know what you can prove—nothing. You see, I own half this country; the majority just don't know it. My family's company helped build up this country since the 1800s, but it's my will that keeps it going. Nearly two-sixths of this country's population work for me, whether they know it or not.

"I've often thought it's a waste of my talents staying in just one city. Someone with your abilities could be very useful to me on a, shall we say, global scale. You could've been a live rich man, instead of a poor dead one," Segel professed while Alex stayed silent.

A minute later the mogul was abruptly and brutally dropped to the ground, unconscious.

After Alex had taken care of Segel, he finally realized they were alone. The driver had vanished, and Alex didn't see a sign of her anywhere. He ran to the end of the driveway and looked in both directions along Greiner Road, but there was no sign of her. Alex concentrated, but he couldn't see, smell, or hear her anywhere. There was some traffic on both sides of the road, but nothing close enough to have picked her up. Alex hated the idea of the girl escaping, but there wasn't anything he could do except call Hill and let him know what happened. "Sonuvabitch," was all he said, suddenly getting a bad feeling this was far from over.

TWENTY-FOUR

TWO DAYS LATER

Western New York had been buzzing about the events of the past ninety-six hours, most unaware that they were all intertwined, like the Gordian Knot. There was the seiche, the vigilante who stopped the Trax, and the arrest of Regino Segel. Footage from both the takedown of the Trax and Segel's arrest had been leaked online. The security cameras from the parking ramp and at the Brookfield Country Club, which line the property, captured everything. After the footage went viral, some metahuman enthusiasts believed two different men handled the situations, while others argued it was the same man. In the days that followed, there had been considerable debate.

As the world moved on, Alex was summoned by Grandmother and took the drive back out to the Reservation to speak with her on a chilly, gray morning. She was sitting in front of her longhouse on a small wooden bench made of logs and branches, nibbling on an apple. "Good morning, my son," she said as Alex approached.

"Morning, ma'am," he answered kindly. Despite being in his early fifties, Alex felt like he was one hundred and eighty.

"Something troubles you," the Medicine Woman said, more a statement and not a question.

"Yeah, you could say that," Alex said while taking a seat on one of the tree stumps in front of the longhouse.

"These are challenging times for you, but have faith you are walking the right path, Grandmother said before taking another small bite.

"That is an understatement, Grandmother," Alex said. Suddenly an icy wind, typical of December or January off of Lake Erie, rose up, blowing leaves and forest debris around, forming a mini whirlwind. Despite wearing his red and black flannel over a tee and a charcoal sleeveless fleece vest, Alex felt chilled. "It's what happened the other day when I arrested Segel," he continued, then told Grandmother all about hearing the voice and the female entity he saw.

"I see," was all she said. With eyes shut, she stayed still and just sat there. For a moment Alex thought she fell asleep on him, bored by the story.

Frustration building, he released it when he yelled out loud, "Is that it?"

Grandmother opened her gray, worn eyes, and gave Alex a look that would have stopped a squad of Marines in their tracks. Pointing a finger at him, she stated "Do not mistake my silence for indifference or being heartless."

Realizing his mouth went on autopilot again, Alex apologized. "I'm sorry, but this has been the most insane, aggravating, and disturbing week, not just for me, but for my parents too. You're the first person I told this to, and I thought when it happened, I was going insane. He looked towards the floor of the forest, at the fallen leaves that had lost their spectacular autumn colors and were now shades of brown and tan, dried out and rustling and crackling underfoot.

"When Shunkaha Wakinyan marked you, he essentially merged his lifeforce with yours. You now carry his warrior and hunter's spirit. Shunkaha Wakinyan can be aggressive and difficult to deal with, but he never does anything without reason. He possesses a warrior's code of honor that he follows without question. Admittedly, this may be difficult to hear, but it appears that after your merging, you may have adopted his traits. His instincts may now be a part of you."

"Jesus Christ," Alex said feeling unnerved more than he already had been. "It's bad enough I'm destined to be some world savior, but now I've got a personality disorder and maybe mentally unstable."

"No, not at all," Grandmother replied while shaking her head. Slightly amused, the Medicine Woman let a small smile across her lips. "What does the word warrior mean to you Alexander," Grandmother asked, her tone sounding more maternal and warmer.

"A fighter or soldier, I guess," Alex answered, sounding despondent.

She shook her head, "No. Our Lakota brothers have a saying, "The true meaning of a warrior is not to destroy, but to heal and protect." This reflects the belief that a warrior's role extends beyond battle to include the safeguarding and nurturing of the community. It's about embodying courage, honor, and selflessness." Then Grandmother raised a point, "You said you saw a female deity that had elements of a deer, rabbit, and mainly an owl?"

Alex nodded slightly, "Yeah, sound familiar?"

"Yes, since you are dealing with Shunkaha Wakinyan I suspect you saw Nokomis."

"Who is she? I never heard of her."

"She, like Shunkaha Wakinyan, is a divine being very few have heard of. She is his lover and one of the few who brings him balance," Grandmother explained as Alex stared at her. "Whereas he is the hunter, warrior, and protector, Nokomis represents wisdom, knowledge, and she is a teacher. Her other traits include fertility, and she is connected to the cycle of life, along with harmony, awareness, and quick thinking."

As Grandmother spoke, she smiled wider. "If you encountered Nokomis believe me this is a good thing. She will provide the balance you will require. Nokomis is the calm to Shunkaha Wakinyan's storm surge, the bard to his fighter."

Grandmother's look changed from stern to loving compassion. "You are going through a great deal, as are your parents, but worry not about them. Reginald and Celeste are stronger than you may think."

Alex was stunned, because he had never mentioned his parents' names and wondered how she knew them. Before he could ask, Grandmother continued, "They and your grandfather all have faith and know you will walk through the upcoming trials and be stronger on the other side."

Alex was about to ask what she meant, when Grandmother quickly pulled herself up, with her staff, which had been leaning against the longhouse. "It is time you must master your most important abilities."

"What's that?" Alex asked, making a mental note to inquire about his parents later. He had come to realize that when Grandmother spoke, she expected immediate results.

Heading back towards the Sanctuary, Grandmother turned, looking over her shoulder and said, "You must forge a link with the Sanctuary that will allow you to go to where you are needed, when you are needed." Alex wondered what was next and how much more he could take, as Grandmother walked on in silence, at her own pace.

In less than five minutes they were back at the Sanctuary, having gone through the mist and fog, despite the temperatures and wind gusts that were still moving. When they reached the holy grounds, Alex saw several animals were there, gathering their strength.

"The two most important powers are the ability to know where you are needed most, which Shunkaha Wakinyan gave you when he marked you," Grandmother said, turning to face Alex and looking him square in the eye. "Now I will help you learn of your second most important power: being able to create portals that will take you to where you're needed." She then continued walking towards a fire pit made of stones and rocks.

Alex just stood there speechless, then asked, "What do you mean?"

"Help an old woman and bring me some logs." She pointed towards a small pile that sat by one of the benches of wood and logs.

Alex respectfully picked up an armful of firewood and brought it over to the stone ring.

While he toted the wood, Grandmother continued, by pulling some kindling and herbs from a belt pouch she wore. "Among your abilities is to control the four natural elements, this you already know."

"Right," Alex said as he began laying the logs in the fire ring. "The other day, and don't ask me how, in some way, I created a blockade of rock and stone, that turned the car on its side, then called up a wind gust so strong it sent a gun from that girl's hand flying across Segel's front lawn."

Grandmother just smiled at Alex "You are already

showing progress, and that is good, but your hand was forced. Right now, you are like an infant taking its first steps, learning to walk. In your case it is much more dangerous, because you do not know what you are doing and can cause more harm than you can imagine."

Alex took Grandmother's words to heart. "I understand." After laying down the last log, he continued, "The other night, after Segel was taken into custody by the Feds, I spent most of the day making things official with Hill. I still have some training to complete for my certifications. Then, I had to fill out the reports about what happened at Segel's house. I had a lot of time to think, and I realized I need to gain real control."

Grandmother just nodded slowly and said, "Good, you realize this already, that is your first step."

"So, what's next?"

"Now, now we begin." Grandmother waved her hand over the kindling, with her palm spread out and a shower of sparks burst from her hand, raining down. Soon a crackling fire was alive. Alex watched in awe, then sat like an attentive student, absorbed in what Grandmother was teaching him.

"Before you can learn to create a portal, you need to master controlling fire because fire is the tool that will create the portals." She continued to explain. "Like a great many things fire is a tool used in many ways; we cook with it, heat our homes, light the darkness, and you my son will master it, but first we need to forge your link with the Sanctuary."

From her belt Grandmother pulled a curved knife, about four inches long, with a handle made of deer bone. She unsheathed it and came closer to Alex. "Men have become blood brothers when circumstances dictate it, in a sense that's what has to happen here."

Alex had an idea of what was needed. He came closer to

Grandmother, mentally bracing himself. "Alright, let's do it." He presented his right hand to her, as she raised the curved blade over lowering it to his palm, then made a three-inch slice across his hand. Out of instinct Alex braced himself for the passing pain, then balled up his fist as Grandmother put the knife away. Alex let the blood flow for a moment, then asked, "Now what?"

"Lay your blood in front of the fire," Grandmother said as she pointed with her staff towards the stones that made up the circle.

Alex had an idea of what she meant as he walked in front of the fire. He noticed some of the animals watching him: a bear, several birds, and one particularly large wolf who was black and gray with ice blue eyes. Alex recognized the wolf from his last visit.

Alex bent over, lowering down to one knee and then placed his palm, which was coated in his blood, on the stone that was closest to the fire. He felt the heat of the fire on the stone and was surprised how quickly it had heated up.

To Alex's shock, the flames flared up as if a jet of natural gas had been pumped into them, and he almost fell backward from the shock. He maintained his balance, crouched in front of the fire, as the flames reached out toward him of their own accord. Taking on a life of their own, they began circling counterclockwise, starting from the right side of Alex's palm, moving up to where his thumb was, then spiraling upwards, becoming narrower and narrower. Once the tip of the flame was at eye level with Alex, it almost seemed as if the fire was staring at him.

Alex felt like he was being looked at by a wild animal, that was making a connection with a human. On the one hand, Alex was almost tempted to reach out and touch it with his free hand, but on the other the voice of common sense was telling him, *DON'T STUPID! IT'S FIRE!*

Suddenly the tip of the spiral jetted out almost like a snake, striking its prey, and it went right into Alex's right hand. The flame enveloped his hand, just past his wrist, and at first his normal initial reaction was fear, but he wasn't being burnt, let alone feeling any pain.

The flames enveloped Alex's hand, but they didn't burn him or his clothing. He raised his arm, looking at his palm, and to his astonishment, the fresh wound healed itself, almost as if his skin was self-sealing. Alex felt the heat, and it almost seemed as if the fire was integrating itself into his body on a cellular level, as if it were passing through every pore in his skin.

As he stood up, Alex turned to Grandmother, who'd been standing in silence watching everything that took mere moments. "What's happening?" he asked.

"You are becoming one with the Earth itself my son," Grandmother said. "Think of it this way," she explained, starting by waving her staff in the direction of the animals that surrounded them "Yes, you will be able to command the elements, but never forget it's more of a partnership. We live with our animal brothers and sisters, but our place is to be their guardians and the guardians of the planet. Remember we are not their masters, there are those who forget this, when they learn the truth it's too late for them."

Grandmother's tone suddenly changed, becoming more authoritative, instructive. "What you need to do, my son," using her staff she pointed to a space, to the side that was between them then continued, "Concentrate on a place you want to be, don't think about it just the first place you can think of that comes to mind."

Alex did as told, and suddenly the flames surrounding his hand turned various shades of green. Looking at his hand from all sides, puzzled, yet amazed he then asked, "Now what?"

"Extend your hand, use the flame and draw a circle of fire." Alex continued to follow her instructions, and the green flames jetted from his hand outward. A circle of fire formed, but it didn't dissipate, staying in place, hanging in midair.

Grandmother then said, "Inside the circle draw the land and the water, mountains and rivers."

Alex continued to draw, and when his hand reached the starting point, he began to go horizontally within the ring, then moved upward, forming an image of a pair of mountains, one larger than the other. At the other side of the circle, he doubled back and began to go downwards, forming what looked like a body of water, a river at an angle coming out of the mountains. He then went backward, up toward the mountains, forming a second parallel river at the same angle and finished the drawing at the point he had started.

Alex just watched the image hover in place, forgetting what else was happening or the fact that his right hand was still on fire, with green flame. His head began to shake back and forth a little bit in disbelief.

Grandmother then commanded, "Think about where you want to be, think about what came to your mind, concentrate."

Alex thought of the first place that came to his mind and at first the image inside the circle didn't do anything, but as Alex focused harder the image jetted into flame again. After the flare up died down the image inside the circle had changed from what Alex had drawn to Marie's cottage in West Seneca.

Ohmigod, was the only thought Alex had. He couldn't understand why Marie's was the first place to come to mind, but he'd given up asking questions by this point. Grandmother just smiled.

"Well done," she said.

"What's next?" Alex asked, his tone revealing he was punch-drunk.

"Think about what you want to do. You are looking to go to this place." Grandmother added. "It must be a very special place if it came to your mind so quickly."

Alex concentrated, the circle grew larger, becoming bigger than a doorway, large enough for Alex to jump through. Without a word, Alex cautiously reached out towards the circle with his left hand. After a moment of hesitation, he finally reached through, with his arm, and realizing it was safe, Alex stepped all the way through. He found himself in the heart of West Seneca, in front of Marie's cottage.

"I don't believe..." was all Alex could mutter when he heard someone yelling from two houses away.

As Alex stood in front of the cottage he heard from across the street, "Mister your arm!" A pair of women walking their dogs in front of the school saw Alex and were freaking out.

Oh boy. Alex realized he'd better get back to Grandmother, once he saw them.

"Look at his eyes, Maddie," the shorter, white-haired housewife, walking her husky practically screamed, while pointing at Alex. He had forgotten about his eyes changing shape when using his powers.

"It's all right, ladies," he said then focused on Grandmother and the Sanctuary. Once Alex had Grandmother in sight, he turned back to the dogwalkers, and said, "Trust me ladies, everything's all right," then leapt into the portal, leaving the women and their dogs confused.

———

For the rest of the morning and well into the afternoon Alex practiced with his new abilities. Grandmother watched him repeatedly draw the portal image over until he had it down in five seconds flat.

After that Alex learned the basics in fire manipulation. Grandmother had him create streams of fire from his hands, as if he were a living flamethrower. "Remember the elements will respond to your will, so you must master being in harmony with your emotions and the elements. They will respond to your feelings."

Thinking back, Alex thought about when he forced the car on its side and the wind gust, those were reactionary, self-preservation moments. "So, if my temper gets out of hand or Shunkaha Wakinyan's influence takes over, in a very bad way," he began saying, emphasizing his words with a rolling hand gesture, "Things can go more than go bad in a New York moment?"

Grandmother looked mournful. "Correct my son. You have no idea how grave things can become."

"Okay, let's practice," he said trying to sound confident, more for himself than anyone else.

At first, Alex just jet brief bursts of fire from his hands upwards, which was an incredible sensation. With palms outstretched and upright, his hands were on fire, but Alex only felt the heat without being burned. Later, things got out of control when Alex put a little too much oomph into his willpower and launched a stream of fire almost forty feet. This frightened most of the animals, causing them to scatter in search of protection. Grandmother immediately cast a protection spell to block the fire and shield the Sanctuary.

Once Alex realized what he'd done he willed the fires to snuff themselves out. "My god I can't believe I did that," Alex felt totally embarrassed and dejected. Then suddenly he became more upset at himself. He took it harder than he should have, silently cursing himself the way he always did whenever he made a mistake, even if he was inexperienced at something. It was a habit he had since he was a teenager.

"This is what I referred to earlier," Grandmother said sternly. "You have so much potential within you to be the greatest guardian the Earth has ever seen, but at the same time you also have enough potential to rip the planet apart and kill every living being on it."

That was a moment of truth for Alex. Alex took the entire situation seriously, ever since Wolfhart showed up, but seeing what he had just done, and hearing Grandmother now, was too much for Alex.

Alex felt a familiar sensation in his core. He'd broken out in a sweat that poured from every pore on his head. Despite the chilly October temperatures, he was burning up, and it wasn't from the fire. He walked away from the Medicine Woman, who just watched him step in between some trees and bushes. Alex breathed heavily through his mouth, as he braced himself, leaning over, holding himself up on his knees, then moments later, everything in his stomach rushed out in four massive heaves of stomach acid and bile.

After things settled, Alex sat down on the nearest tree stump before he collapsed. Grandmother slowly joined him taking the stump next to him. "It will be alright my son, no one was harmed, the animals are all fine, the grounds are protected." She placed her hand on his shoulder attempting to reassure Alex.

After a few moments wrapped up in the fog of his thoughts Alex spoke slowly "I, I…. I don't think I can do this," he said already sounding defeated and the man's mission hadn't even begun.

"Alexander," Grandmother began, "You have proven your worth, otherwise the Sacred Circle would never have blessed you with your gifts."

"Gifts, blessings?" He looked at Grandmother with a mixture of dread and anger. "It's funny how one person's 'gifts' can be another's curse. No one asked if I was okay with all this. I mean I have, had my own plans, ideas for my life, and I hate being controlled, manipulated the way you're all doing," he said with the first real anger he'd been able to release since this all began.

"I do not know why you and your family were chosen to be the guardians, but it was for a reason. I've no idea what that reason is or was, but I do know you are stronger than you believe. Have faith in yourself because I know your grandfather, your parents, and I do. Even Shunkaha Wakinyan does as well."

TWENTY-FIVE

In Western New York's underworld there's an establishment known as 'Leisureland', near Model City, N.Y., and the infamous Love Canal, in the Northtowns. The establishment offers metahuman criminals a variety of services from strip clubs, to body rub parlors, and considerably more. For additional fees, specialized services can be provided: refuge for someone on the run, until they can make it to the criminal version of the 'underground railroad'. This is where Macaria had been hiding for the past four days.

Macaria had been lounging around her luxury suite waiting for Hasting Segel, Regino's uncle, to show up after she sent him a message of what happened. Ordering room service, relaxing in the Jacuzzi hot tub, and basically decompressing, all while trying to learn anything she could about Segel's arrest and the man who stopped them, but getting little accomplished.

Even though Macaria had been enjoying the amenities offered, such as massage sessions and gourmet meals, she'd been getting anxious, and after three days the enforcer and "hench-woman" was borderline frantic. It'd gotten to the point where Macaria's paranoia needed reigning in. Any time there was a knock at the door, she answered it, armed.

On day four, Macaria finally heard the knock she'd been waiting for. She slipped her bathrobe on, cautiously stood off to the side at the door, and looked through the peephole, while thumbing back the hammer on her back-up, a modified Berretta, then felt a sense of relief when she saw Hastings standing there.

Macaria opened the door, as she put the gun in the pocket of her robe. "Glad you could finally make it," Macaria said with some pent up hostility in her voice.

Hastings marched through the door like an invading general and returned some hostility of his own. "Just be glad I got here as fast as I did. Thanks to that idiot nephew of mine, things are fucked up across the company. Stockholders are getting anxious." Then he pulled out a personal cigar case from his topcoat's pocket. "Of course, reporters are dogging me. Hell, took me almost ninety minutes to make sure I lost them from the airport before I made my way here."

As Macaria closed the door, a six-foot-six distinguished bald man entered. His rugged, distinguished appearance was marked by a strong jawline and a well-groomed Verdi beard. His presence was commanding, often conveying intensity and authority, but he continued to rant, sounding more like a Union leg breaker than a billionaire industrialist and C.E.O.

"I'm in Tokyo, working several deals, when that moron makes his big power play, forcing me to reschedule my meetings with the Japanese government, as well as the Oyabun, head of the whole fucking Yakuza." Tossing his black topcoat on the four-poster bed, the industrialist continued to shout, "Now Regino's in a federal detention center, possibly facing domestic terrorist charges, you're on the run, and I'm in the fucking dark." He emphasized his point by pointing right at Macaria. "Tell me exactly everything that happened and don't leave out one fucking detail!" He slid a gold cigar cutter and a matching lighter from his blue sportscoat, trimmed one of the Havannas he carried, then lit up, before sitting down on the loveseat, across from the wall mounted flat screen.

Macaria sat on the edge of the bed, staring at the real power behind Segel International, bracing herself for the coming storm, then began. "Okay," she said, then took a moment to gather her thoughts and recall what happened. "It all started about a week and a half ago..." Once she finished her story, the blue-haired, Texas native just said, "So?"

After taking a drawn out drag on his cigar Hastings said, "That's some story," then let out a growl of frustration, stood up, then began pacing around the floor due to his angry, nervous energy that had to be released. "As smart as he is, that kid always had more balls than brains."

A moment or two of uncomfortable silence, where Hastings considered everything, he was told, pointed at Macaria with his left fingers, holding his cigar in-between them and said, "I don't blame you. Regino made this mess, and he can clean it himself."

Macaria felt a sense of relief knowing she would be taken care of.

"You'll be protected since you've done right by us before, but there's no way you could have anticipated dealing with some superhuman freak."

Macaria said, "I appreciate that." It felt a little peculiar for her having gone from one employer who she shared an NSA relationship with to essentially his superior, who was a bit older, and possibly more dangerous to a degree. "So now what?" she asked.

Hastings stopped moving around like a caged animal, turned, and looked out the window facing northwest, towards the defunct Model City. "Right now, we clean up the mess my nephew left. We don't have any choice in the matter because this is going to be a legal nightmare for all of us." Turning back to face his employee, Hastings continued. "First off, I saw Regino yesterday, and things don't look good. He's looking at a possible domestic terrorist charge, only behind Timothy McVeigh and Oklahoma City. But right now, that doesn't matter to him at all."

"What do you mean?"

Hastings took a moment, then admitted something very few knew. "I've always known he wasn't all there, something was always off about him ever since he was a boy, but the idea of facing a possible life sentence in a federal institution didn't faze him."

Macaria had seen the man face down a room full of military officers during a contract negotiation, but she never seen him as distressed as he was now. "Yesterday we met with our lawyers, and they told us the Department of Justice, the FBI, Homeland Security, the Cattaraugus County District Attorney, and the Tribal Council are all investigating him, and if convicted he'll be lucky to get life. Regino just sat there, smiling."

Macaria saw Hastings was unnerved and forced herself to ask, "What did he say?"

Looking alarmed, Hasting told her what happened. "He said he's ready for this and prepared himself. Also, he wants that bastard, referring to the hero, dead. He told me he wants me to use our resources to find out everything we can about him, then kill his entire family and all his friends, but leave him for the last."

An unearthly chill entered the room, and Macaria felt a sudden shiver go down her spine. She knew Segel could be violent, was vindictive as hell, but hearing this made Macaria realize that he was at a level she never imagined. "Do you think we can do it?", she asked.

"Right now, I'm not even sure if we should try," Hastings said.

Macaria just shook her head in disbelief and asked the only thing she could ask, "Now what?"

"I want you to lay low here for a few more days, I'll send Rollins to collect you. He's wrapping up talks with that group from Quebec and should be back here in forty-eight hours. From my understanding, the authorities have issued an A.P.B. for you but don't have many details, so as long as you keep your head, and listen to me," Hastings said, standing back up over Macaria, capturing her complete attention, "you do what I say, leave my nephew to me, and everything will be fine."

Macaria stood up to look Hastings in the eye, and stepped right up to him, invading his personal space, then asked with a wicked look on her face, "What about him, the 'hero'?"

"Don't get me wrong I'm not opposed to the idea of killing him, but he stopped a bombing on an Indian Reservation, where women, children, and seniors were close by. If we kill him, we could be making a martyr, and that's the last thing we need."

TWENTY-SIX

The following Saturday there was a meeting in the Harlows' backyard; assembled were Alex, his parents, Wolfhart, Orsen, and Marie. To a casual observer the family and friends were enjoying the beautiful fall afternoon, with the crackling fire in the center of a black, steel fire pit, surrounded by six high back Adirondack style chairs, with a pair of matching huge square shaped tables between them.

This was more like a war council convening.

Alex was the only one standing, practically hovering over Marie as she compared the official state copies, which had finally arrived at her office, to Wolfhart's copies. Marie finally declared, "Alex, as far as my agency is concerned, these documents are legitimate copies Mr. Dorset obtained, how, I've no idea," she said glancing in the P.I.'s direction. "As far as I can tell Mr. Wolfhart is your grandfather." As she finished speaking, Marie slid her reading glasses off, placing them into her purse. "Undoubtedly, you already knew that based on everything you've told me," she said with a look that shot a dagger or two at Alex for not telling her the whole story sooner. "But at least now, in the eyes of New York State it's official."

Alex said, "Thanks, Marie, I appreciate the confirmation. I really didn't need it but at least that's out of the way." Alex placed his hand on her shoulder looking down at her.

She looked back up at him and smiled and for a moment the two of them realized something was building.

As much as Alex wanted to keep the moment going, he knew he couldn't, then asked, "All right, now what?"

Reggie looked bewildered and his head began to shake back and forth very slightly. Alex realized his father was having trouble comprehending everything.

Alex tried to explain everything that happened at the Sanctuary with Grandmother, but he had a tough time convincing his dad.

"I know what you told us, but I still don't understand what you meant you made a portal of fire," his father said looking a little confused. Then he turned to Wolfhart and asked, "Do you have any idea what he's talking about?"

Shaking his head, Wolfhart answered, "No, no I don't. I never heard of anything like this. All any of our ancestors could tap into were the animal abilities. Alex possesses powers I wasn't aware of." Looking a little sheepishly, Wolfhart admitted, "Grandmother doesn't always tell me everything. For example, I never heard of this female goddess, this Nokomis, and I've lived with these legends my whole life."

"Alex," his mom said, looking up towards her son, who moved closer to the firepit, almost looking like he was leading this discussion. "I don't doubt what you told us, but maybe it would be better if you demonstrated for your father."

Knowing how Reggie could be, Alex agreed. "Okay, Mom," Alex rolled up the sleeves of his red and black, flannel shirt, turned and faced the fire pit. At first, he felt the apprehension he felt back with Grandmother. The natural fear of getting burned was there but Alex told himself you know what you're capable of.

"Alex, what are you doing?" Reggie asked as he started to rise from his deck chair.

Without looking at anybody in the group Alex knew his mother did the same thing, but Wolfhart, even though he hadn't seen Alex master the element of fire, had faith in his grandson's capabilities.

"It's okay everyone, trust me, I know what I'm doing," Alex said as he started to put his right hand towards the fire pit while, at the same time his left hand touched the arrowhead hanging around his neck. Alex felt a charge run through his body from his toes and the bottom of his feet up to his head. It was almost like a mile charge of electricity that didn't hurt him but energized him.

Alex put his hand to the flames. Suddenly, to everyone's astonishment, he raised his right forearm showing that his hand and a portion of his forearm were surrounded by an aura of flame that didn't harm him.

"I don't believe it," Reggie said.

Alex smiled because for one of the few times in his father's life, the man went totally slack jawed.

"Does it hurt?" Marie asked, bolting like a colt from her chair and came up right alongside Alex. She was quickly followed by everyone else, and Alex just smiled.

"No, no I'm fine everyone," he said calmly as he explained what it was like. "The best way I can describe it, it's like this; I feel the heat, the warmth basically, but it doesn't hurt. What Grandmother told me, it's a balance, what I mean is man is meant to live in harmony with the planet and the natural elements, as well as with the animals. Unfortunately, it's something that we've fallen short of as a species. So as much as it looks like I'm controlling the fire, it's more like we're in harmony, it's a tool and as long as I respect the power of nature and don't do anything to harm it then the fire and I'm assuming the other elements will respond to my needs or wishes. According to Grandmother it's the same with air, water, and earth as well."

"What can you do?" Orsen asked.

"Well," sheepishly Alex admitted, "the other day I acted like a human flamethrower, and almost accidentally burned down a section of the Sanctuary."

"Judas Priest," was the only thing Wolfhart could say.

"The first thing that Grandmother had me master was this..." Alex then held his forearm in front of him concentrated and suddenly the flames turned green like they did before, and he saw astonishment grow on his audience's faces.

"Okay, here we go folks," he said. Alex took a few steps to the side to give himself some room, concentrated, and then repeated the ritual for drawing the portal. Once the image was complete, just hovering in mid-air, everyone took a good look at it before Alex did anything else.

"My God," Reggie said.

Wolfhart just shook his head in disbelief. Even though he had seen and done some amazing things as the Red Warrior, this was completely new to him. The others were in a similar state of awe.

Alex's eyes took on the avian appearance, again, but nobody noticed it since everyone was watching the literal fireworks. Alex concentrated and focused on the Sanctuary. A moment later everyone saw the sacred site. In the center of the circle of fire everyone could see the pool of water and the numerous animals taking refuge there.

"Alex?" Celeste asked, "Is that it, the place you told us about?"

"Yeah, Mom," he said, while trying to keep his focus. "Basically, it's like this," he began to explain. "Grandmother told me thanks to Shunkaha Wakinyan I'll know where I'm needed immediately, almost like Grandmother Earth calling nine-one-one, and now creating the portals I'll be able to go from one location to another, as long as it's for a good reason."

"Whattaya mean mate?" Orsen asked.

"If it's to help regarding a disaster, natural or man-made, or protecting someone or something, or to return to the Sanctuary to recover, that's one thing, but it's not a party trick. I can't create a portal to go grocery shopping or run errands. So, no beer runs people," he joked.

"When Grandmother taught you how to create these portals, where was the first place you went to," Wolfhart asked without taking his eyes off the gateway.

"To be perfectly honest," Alex began to sheepishly admit, "Grandmother told me not to think about it, she said to concentrate on the first place that comes to mind."

"Where was that, Alex?" Celeste asked.

After a moment of apprehension, Alex finally told everyone what happened. "After I drew the entry, Marie's cottage came to mind. I went through and I appeared right in front of your house." As Alex turned around to face her the portal flickered out in a green puff. Alex was slightly embarrassed, but he could see more surprise on everyone's face except for Marie who seemed to have more questions.

"Why my cottage?" Marie asked.

"No idea. All I know for certain is Grandmother told me to go with my instincts and your cottage was the first place that came to mind, so I just ran with the ball. Next thing I know I'm there and two of your neighbors, walking their dogs saw me emerge from a green flaming doorway and then dive back through." Alex just looked at Marie. He shook his head and said, "All in all it was a pretty busy afternoon for me," then he laughed.

After answering more questions from everybody, which took about another half hour or so, the Harlows invited the others to stay for dinner. So, while Alex grilled hamburgers and sausages, he answered questions and discussed his plans now, since his normal life in a sense was over.

"Tell me," Orson asked Alex after taking a sip of his bottled beer, "You gonna get a fancy costume like your grandfather and your mother had?" he joked.

"Hell, no," Alex said tending to the burgers and sausages. He shook his head slightly as he continued "After what happened at the reservation and being caught on camera footage already, I figure the secrets out."

"What's that mean?" Orsen asked.

"Boils down to this," Alex said while looking at Orson square in the eye. "I've accepted what's happening, I've accepted the fact this is out of my hands and people are counting on me, and I just don't mean my parents anymore. I don't know what's gonna happen and I don't know what else I'm capable of or what I'll be facing, but the one thing I can guarantee you," Alex paused, put his hand on Orsen's shoulder then said, "there is no way in hell I'm running around in a silly costume and a cape." Then he started laughing again.

Orson shook his head and started laughing as well. "Yeah, I can kind of see where you're coming from. Granted there are some sharp costumes that people are wearing out there."

Alex couldn't argue the point; there were several costumed heroes in some villains that had pretty sharp fashion sense, and Alex began to wonder where some of them got their costumes. It's not like Macy's, Target,

Walmart, or even Amazon have their own sections for ordering real life costumes.

"Seriously," Alex said as he began taking the food off of the grill and putting it on a serving platter, "there were a lot of witnesses who saw me in action and I'm gonna be out there a lot to practice, cause I'm going to need it plus which I'm now a special officer now, officially so I don't have a choice in the matter really."

They turned back to the fire pit area where his dad and Wolfhart were sitting discussing matters and talking history particularly about when he saw Ojistah in action as Wildrun.

Hearing the two of them talk about her, reminded Alex of something he needed to discuss with Orson. "I don't know if this ever came up with him," Alex said and shifted his head towards Wolfhart, "but I wanna hire you for a job."

"What is it?" Orson asked, confused.

As Celeste and Marie came out of the house carrying glasses with ice and more sodas and beers, Alex explained, "I want you to find my mother." Alex said. "I want, no wait," and he stopped himself. "I need to find her since I have questions that need answers and only she can provide them."

Orson slowly nodded his head. "Okay, we can talk in a couple of days, cause I have some business out of town first, but when I get back, we'll talk, okay?"

"Sounds doable."

After dinner Alex grabbed his car keys since he had to drive Marie back home. Her car was still detained downtown with everyone else's. He came back into the foyer and overheard Marie talking to Celeste. As she packed up her work bag, Marie thanked the Harlows for their hospitality. "I can't tell you what a pleasure it is to finally meet you," she said while they were headed towards the front door.

"To be honest," Celeste said, "I can't thank you enough

for helping Alex out. I know it's been an ordeal for him, but having someone like you supporting him has been nothing short of a blessing." Celeste then looked at her son who was standing right there, then a mischievous look ran across her face and Alex recognized it immediately. "And of course he can always use more friends, especially smart ones like yourself." Celeste turned to Alex and asked, "So what does this make three or four?"

Alex returned fire. "You see, Marie, in our family, if we like you, we pick on you, and normally I'd say something to my mother at this point, but being she is so short she can give an overhand left to the nuts, so I'm not gonna risk it."

"Very funny mister," his mother said.

"Alex," Marie began to scold.

With a big smirk on his face, Alex knew when it was time to sound a retreat. He placed his hand on Marie's shoulder and started to guide her out the door. "Well, I'd love to stay here and verbally spar with you, Mom, but I have to get this young lady back home."

Celeste watched from the doorway as Alex opened the car door for Marie, feeling both apprehensive and hopeful. As she headed back to join Reggie and their guests, she finally noticed something building between Alex and Marie. She had no idea where it would lead, but she hoped for the best, especially with Alex's new responsibilities.

———

The short drive through South Buffalo and West Seneca was a lot more pleasant than the last time. Alex realized it was a comfortable silence with the only sound in the car was the CD player playing a Frank Sinatra concert. At a red light he glanced at Marie who had her eyes shut and was leaning to her side resting her head on her hand.

"Tired?" Alex asked as they reached a red light.

"No, not really," Marie answered. "I was just thinking."

"Anything serious?"

"I'm not sure," Marie said. "I'm just wondering what all this is gonna mean for you. I saw that footage from downtown, and you told us about what happened on the reservation, but natural disasters that's something else entirely." As they turned onto her street Marie sat up and got to her point. "I guess what I'm wondering is how will you stop a natural disaster?"

Letting out a drawn-out sigh, as they pulled into the blacktop driveway, Alex admitted, "I don't know. I mean it depends on whether I can, or if in some cases I should."

"What do you mean?"

Alex turned the engine off then explained. "Grandmother explained to me that the planet itself is going through a healing process, but it's going to take time, because of the damage humans have caused and even though the healing process has begun, we're still doing more damage. You know how when you're sick with a bad case of the flu or something, and you'll get a fever or nausea?" Alex asked. Marie nodded, understanding what he meant. "You have to ride out the sickness before you get better, well, it's like that and some of these natural disasters are gonna have to run their course."

"So, what exactly is expected of you?" Marie asked, leaning a little closer to him.

"I'm not sure. I know protecting as many people as possible is a priority, and stopping any ecological disasters is also high on that list. I've a feeling Grandmother or the Sacred Circle will let me know, because I don't know if 'on the job training' is going to be enough."

Marie changed the subject. "Seems I still owe you for the other night." Alex became a little confused and was about to say something when she said, "Care to come in for a drink?"

"Sure, I've a feeling I can use it."

A moment later they were inside, Alex in the front room examining one of the three paintings hanging on the light blue walls, as Marie was in the kitchen. "I like these paintings," Alex said.

Marie strolled in behind him, carrying a bottle of white wine and a glass in one hand and a drinking glass filled with hard cider in the other. "Thank you, I painted those myself. Here you go," she said handing the hard cider to Alex. "I have a feeling you're a bourbon man, but also hard cider will do."

"Thank you," he said, surprised at how insightful Marie was. "How'd you know?"

"Just a feeling I guess." She took a sip, then offered a seat.

"Where'd you paint those?" he asked pointing at the landscapes.

"San Diego, the one on the right is from Old Town," she said as they sat on her love seat. "It's a part of town that's a historical park of how the area was back in the 1800s. That's the First San Diego Courthouse and the Colorado House, now the Wells Fargo History Museum."

"You got a real talent there. Ever paint anything around here?"

"Just the back yard. The light around here is really good, weather depending, of course," Marie said. After taking another sip of wine, she placed her glass on the coffee table in front of them. "Alex, when you said you were marked by that God, Shun... oh, I cannot pronounce his name,"

"Shunkaha Wakinyan, it means wolf with wings of thunder," Alex said.

"Well, when you said you were marked by him what did you mean exactly?"

"The best way I can explain it's like this, when I went on the first spiritual trip, back in our living room, and I don't know how else to describe it, Shunkaha Wakinyan stared me down, then with his claw swiped at me, specifically my chest. Even though my body was here, in the real world," Alex made air quotes to emphasize his point, "And I didn't feel anything, but when I came back, I found a massive set of claw marks on my chest."

"How did this happen?"

"I don't know. All I can tell you is what Grandmother told me. Shunkaha Wakinyan and I are somehow connected, and that some of his traits are now in my personality. I don't know exactly what that means, but I know that some of my qualities have changed a bit."

"What do you mean?" Marie asked with a new sense of concern.

"As Grandmother put it," Alex began to say as Marie turned closer towards him on the love seat. "According to Grandmother, Shunkaha Wakinyan's a hunter, a warrior, and he is not one that you would want to piss off."

"I see," Marie said pulling back a little bit, which Alex noticed immediately.

"Well, not entirely. What I mean is, I recently saw a female goddess and Grandmother explain to me who she is." Then he explained his encounter with Nokomis and what she represents. "It was really something between the two of them, and I don't think I can fully describe what it was like, either encounter that is."

As they continued talking about Alex's experiences with the deities and everything that happened at the Sanctuary, Marie placed her hand on top of Alex's and suddenly he felt his heart rate go faster.

"Alex," Marie began, "I was wondering…" She paused, almost looking self-conscious or ashamed, then looked down, away from his gaze.

Wondering what his host wanted, Alex placed his left hand under her chin and said, "It's okay, what?"

Looking him in the eye she asked, "I, I was wondering if I could see…it?"

"It," he said, thinking for a moment, then it hit him like a slap to the back of the head. "Oh, my scars?"

"Yes, only if you're all right with showing me," she said, backpaddling, now fully embarrassed.

"It's okay," Alex said as he stood up. "I showed Mom and Dad, and Wolfhart just after it happened." He began unbuttoning his shirt, then took off his tank top undershirt, then stood before her.

Marie examined the scar, much larger than she had imagined. It started at Alex's sternum, ran over his right pectoral, curved to the left, and continued down his stomach before it ended. "Ohmigod," was the only thing Marie could utter. Out of instinct she stood up and reached out with her right hand, tentatively, almost as if she was about to put her hand in a fire. She looked up into Alex's eyes, her lips parted as though about to ask another question, and Alex just nodded while smiling a little smile.

Alex felt a rush that charged through his whole body when Marie reached closer and touched the scar on his chest then her fingers glided downward following the shape. She was about to pull her hand away when Alex reached with his right hand, stopped her and kept it in place. Looking Marie square in the eye, Alex raised his left hand caressed the right side of her face and brushed her hair over her shoulder.

They stared into each other's eyes, neither positive how they'd arrived at this moment, but desire turned into a hunger, that for Alex began to feel insatiable, and before either one could say or think, he followed his instincts and kissed Marie with a passion he never felt before, and she never received before.

The couple gave into their feelings and embraced each other. Alex nuzzled her neck and took her in his arms, as Marie wrapped her arms around him. The passion was running through the two of them like a herd of wild horses running on the plains, and they fully gave in to their desires.

"Alex," Marie started to say.

He stopped, pulled his head away and looked her in the eye. "I'm sorry, is it too much? Do you want me to stop?"

They were both breathing heavily at this point and Marie caressed Alex's face. "No, no I don't." I just wanted to make sure we were both ready for this," almost sounding as if she needed reassurance.

"I know I'm a bit older than you are, and we can stop anytime you want to, just say the word.""No," Marie said as a smile came across her face and she embraced the moment, kissing Alex again.

EPILOGUE

One-week later Alex was at the Southgate Plazza, with his parents and Marie, finishing dinner at a convenient location for everyone, the shopping center being four blocks from Homeward Angels office and less than five minutes from Marie's cottage.

After their relationship turned the page, Alex and Marie thought dinner with the Harlows would be a safe way for his parents to get to know the woman in their son's life, so at Marie's suggestion they met for dinner, where even though everything went fine, Alex felt naturally uneasy.

After Alex asked for the check, his dad asked, "Any word when you're going back to work?"

"No," Alex said. "Last message I got from Allan, our building's supposed to be inspected in another week or so, but the company and the state are making arrangements with the Department of Labor for emergency benefits."

"That's good," Reggie said, then he asked Marie, "Do you work downtown a lot?"

"No, Mr. Harlow," she said shaking her head. "I work out of the West Seneca office, right down on Union, here."

Celeste jumped in reminding Reggie, "You remember, Alex told us Marie's office is at Main and Union, across from the library."

Reggie sat there for a moment trying to recall, then it hit him. "That's right." Alex looked a little awkwardly in Marie's direction.

"Alex, you didn't say what Grandmother and Mr. Wolfhart had you doing today," Celeste transitioned the conversation.

"Ah yeah, well, today Grandmother had me work with learning about the water abilities. We started slow with me creating a jet of water, like a firehose, then a whirlpool, finally a geyser."

As the waitress brought the check, Alex realized she caught the tail end of the conversation, then handed over his debit card with the check.

The young waitress nodded, taking his card up to the register.

"I think it's best certain conversations stay private," Alex said.

"Agreed," Celeste seconded.

Marie and Reggie agreed without any disagreement.

————

Outside the restaurant, Alex and Marie were waiting because Celeste was in the ladies' room and Reggie waited for her inside out of pure instinct. Alex stared down at Marie, just smiling when she asked, "I wondered about your father before…"

Seeing where she was headed, Alex explained. "Yeah, sometimes Dad forgets things and we have to remind him. It used to happen occasionally, but in the past couple of years it's gotten a little more frequent. He has a lot of good days, and can remember things from years ago, but more recent events he struggles with."

"Oh, I'm sorry," Marie said awkwardly, then placed her hand on Alex's.

Caressing her face with his free hand, he said, "It's okay, I mean it sucks but it's not like you did anything."

Before they could continue, Reggie opened the door and he and Celeste came out disrupting the moment.

"Looks like we interrupted something," Celeste joked.

Before Alex could say anything, an earsplitting alarm rang out from around the corner of the plaza, and without thinking he ran down the sidewalk to see what was happening, with Marie right behind him.

Alex looked down the length of the rest of the plaza and towards the next corner he saw a jewelry store being raided. He recognized the thieves, a group of dangerous females calling themselves The Triangle: The Bengal, a feline female hybrid; Jackdaw, a flyer with razor-like wings; and Shark-girl, a crossbred woman with the traits of a great white shark. No one knew their origins, but somehow, they came together and raised hell wherever they went, not caring what they did or who they hurt.

Alex turned to Marie, giving her a direct order, "Go back, get my parents into Christies, and call 911, now!" Instinctively he reached for the arrowhead.

Marie grabbed his arm. "What do you think you're doing?" she demanded to know.

"Someone could get hurt or killed with those maniacs, I can stop them."

"You could also get hurt or killed," she pointed out.

Alex's eyes morphed into their avian appearance, making him look alien again. Seeing his parents starting to head in their direction, Alex yelled out loud, "GO INSIDE! THERE'S A ROBBERY IN PROGRESS! CALL 911!"

Everyone along the front side of the plaza heard Alex shouting. He then focused on Marie. "I have a job to do."

She began begging. "Your job is to protect the environment, not stop thieves."

Then he reminded her, "I'm also now a deputized officer," and unzipping his vest he showed her his gold badge. "It's official, besides," he continued, while pulling out a box of waterproof matches from his jeans. "They won't be ready for me." Alex then leaned in close to Marie, held her head in his free hand and kissed her. "It'll be all right," he said, then he struck a match against his thumbnail.

The flame ignited, and he took a few steps away, smiled at Marie, then his parents, who were still outside watching them, as Alex willed the little flame to grow and expand, overtaking his left hand. Then he placed his hands together and both hands had flaming auras surrounding them.

With a sound of renewed confidence in his voice, Alex said, "This won't take long," then smiled at Marie, finally adding, "Hey, you know what?"

Unsure how take it all in, Marie just said, "What?"

"I love you," and like that Alex whirled around and ran towards the trouble.

Marie, now knowing how Alex felt, smiled as a feeling of joy and excitement overtook her.

Reggie and Celeste caught up with her, and Celeste asked, "What's happening? Where's Alex?"

Marie, following her orders, grabbed Celeste's arm, leading her back to the restaurant. "There's trouble, and Alex is handling it. But he wants us to call the police and stay inside."

"What kind of trouble?" Reggie demanded to know, debating going on to see what was happening or following the women.

"I'll tell you everything, but we need to go, and trust me,

Mr. Harlow, Alex can handle himself," Marie answered with a huge smile on her rosy cheeked face.

———

As he turned the corner, Alex built speed, running at almost twenty miles per hour, avoiding anyone on the pavement, running the length of the plaza. The alarm was beyond deafening as he got closer, but like with the UV spectrum, if he concentrated on what he needed to do, he got past the sound.

Just ahead of him, the feline, brown, white, and black fur covered Bengal, came leaping out of the storefront window, which Alex saw had been shattered inwards, and he heard her yell, "Hurry up you two, we got what we came for!'

Jackdaw flew out the window, pulling up. "Suits me, no room in there for me to maneuver." Then she suddenly spread open her black, metallic wings and unleashed a barrage of explosive, feather-like flechettes on the parking lot, keeping bystanders at bay.

"Sharkgirl, get out here," Bengal ordered.

Finally, the amphibious, ever smiling, grey and black skinned female with gills along her neck and claws to match her teeth emerged, asking, "Must we? There's a pretty clerk in there, I'd like to carve her up!"

Taking in everything as he ran, Alex yelled, "Hey Triangle," then saw all three women look at him coming closer, at an unbelievable speed. "Today's not a good day to be a bad guy!" He leapt in the air, gesturing as to throw a superman punch with his flaming right fist, then unleashed hell in the form of a fiery burst that showed the Triangle, who saw themselves as the top predators of land, sea, and air, there was a new alpha predator, and he was the Rainbow Warrior, Alex Harlow.

Don't miss out on your next favorite book!

———

THANK YOU FOR READING

Did you enjoy this book?

We invite you to leave a review at the website of your choice, such as Goodreads, Amazon, Barnes & Noble, etc.

DID YOU KNOW THAT LEAVING A REVIEW...

- Helps other readers find books they may enjoy.
- Gives you a chance to let your voice be heard.
- Gives authors recognition for their hard work.
- Doesn't have to be long. A sentence or two about why you liked the book will do.

ABOUT THE AUTHOR

Adopted and raised in Buffalo, N.Y., C.G. Eberle began writing at the age of five, when he wrote & drew his own comic books, but fully embraced writing in high school, starting with his school's newspaper, then a few years later got the idea for his first real story, inspired by the television series *Kolchak; the Nightstalker*.

While studying to become an English teacher, he began writing his first mystery *Family Ties*, which was published in 2013, then followed by *Family Plots, Family Education, & Killer Holidays*.

Having been sidetracked the past few years, C.G. is getting back on track with a rewrite of his first book, drawing from his own biological heritage, and now has begun work on the next anthology in his John Seraph mystery series, as well as having four new story ideas he's working on at this time.

Inspired by legendary author Robert B. Parker & his mentor, mystery author Lissa Marie Redmond, C.G. is also an gifted cook, avid reader, skilled researcher, Broadway enthusiast, and comic book collector/historian.

https://cavillier1970.wixsite.com/buffaloamateursleuth/

https://www.facebook.com/profile.php?id=
61572177617081

ALSO BY C.G. EBERLE